#9 Boo Who?

Look for these books
in the Bad News Ballet series:

Bad News Ballet

#9 Boo Who?

Jahnna N. Malcolm

AN
APPLE
PAPERBACK

SCHOLASTIC INC.
New York Toronto London Auckland Sydney

ISBN 0-590-43397-0

12 11 10 9 8 7 6 5 4 3 2 1   0 1 2 3 4 5/9

Printed in the U.S.A.   40

First Scholastic printing, October 1990

*For Blanche and Julian Maddox
with love*

#9 Boo Who?

Chapter One

It was a cold October night in Deerfield, Ohio. A pale yellow moon was shining down on five girls who were huddling together on the fire escape of the civic auditorium. Each girl was dressed in a black leotard and tights, with a black cape tied around her neck and little black bat ears perched on top of her head. The five friends were from the Deerfield Academy of Dance and their costumes were for the Academy's brand-new ballet, *Dracula*.

Inside the auditorium, rehearsal was still going on. Every now and then the orchestra would stop playing and the voice of the director could be heard, barking orders to the dancers. But the five friends had already

1

performed their dance and were waiting to practice the curtain call.

Zan Reed, a tall, thin, fifth-grader, sat under the yellow light of the stage door, holding a book. In a hushed voice she read out loud to her friends, " 'And so, in a single weekend, Tiffany Truenote, teen detective, rescued the frightened town of East Bedford from the clutches of the dreaded Night Prowler.' " Zan closed the book and sighed. "Tiffany Truenote saved an entire town by herself. Isn't that wonderful?"

"I think it's impossible," Gwendolyn Hays said, shoving her wire-rimmed glasses up on her nose. The plump redhead leaned back against the metal step. "I mean, Tiffany's only fifteen. She still lives at home and she can't even drive yet. How can she save an entire town?"

"Tiffany can do anything. She's a genius." Zan's dark eyes flashed in her lovely brown face. The Tiffany Truenote books were her favorite series, and Zan secretly wished she could be just like the teen detective.

"I believe Tiffany could save a town," Mary Bubnik said earnestly. The curly-headed blonde hugged her knees to her chest. "In the last book Zan read us, Tiffany saved an entire stable of Arabian horses. And in the one before that, Tiffany stopped a whole ring of diamond thieves. Why shouldn't she be able to save an entire town?"

2

"You just doubt her because you've never had that kind of an adventure," Zan said to Gwen.

"Yeah," Kathryn McGee agreed, flipping one of her chestnut-colored braids over her shoulder. "Nothing really scary ever happens in dull ol' Deerfield."

"Are you kidding?" Rocky Garcia said as she climbed up the metal ladder leading to the next level of the fire escape. "Haven't you heard about that spooky guy who's going around scaring everyone?"

McGee shook her head and Rocky explained, "He's supposed to be seven feet tall."

"I think if I ever saw somebody seven feet tall, I'd just drop dead on the spot," Mary Bubnik said in her soft southern accent.

Rocky stood on the top rung of the ladder and raised her cape up in the air to look like a giant bat. "He's called the Monster of Mulberry Avenue. But so far he hasn't hurt anyone. He just yells, 'Boo!' "

"Then why is everyone so scared?" Gwen asked.

Rocky hung over the rail and whispered in her best Count Dracula voice, "Wouldn't you be if a seven-foot monster with green hair and a skeleton mask leaped out of a dark alley and yelled 'boo' at you?"

"Don't talk about it!" Mary Bubnik said, huddling close to Zan. "You're giving me goose bumps."

"I haven't even heard about this guy." Gwen

3

cocked her head at Rocky. "How come you know so much about it?"

"From television." Rocky wiggled her eyebrows. "All good bats watch TV."

"When do you find time to watch TV?" McGee asked. "We've been spending every hour after school here at these rehearsals."

The production of *Dracula* was scheduled to open the following weekend and extra rehearsals had been called because of all the special effects being used.

"I saw it on Thad Taylor's TV," Rocky explained. "It's on all the time in his office." Thaddeus Taylor was the civic auditorium's security guard. Every time they went into the theatre, the girls had to stop by his office and announce their names. Thad would check their names off a list he kept on a clipboard by the door, and then let them in the building.

"I don't like talking to him," Mary Bubnik said with a shiver. "He's really weird."

"He's just kind of strange-looking," McGee said. "Being so tall and thin, with that long pointy nose."

"And those tiny, beady eyes," Gwen added.

"It's not how he *looks*," Mary Bubnik said. "It's what he *says*."

"But he doesn't say anything," Rocky pointed out.

"I know," Mary Bubnik said. "And that's what scares me."

4

Gwen waved her hand in the air. "You're scared of everything."

"I think it's just this time of year," Mary Bubnik said, twisting the edge of her cape. "Halloween is a time when weird people put on ugly masks and wander the streets in gory costumes and beg for candy." She shuddered again. "It's all too scary."

"Which reminds me," Gwen said. "Only seven more shopping days till Trick or Treat, and I don't even have my bag yet."

"Well, I don't even have a costume," Rocky said, whipping her cape closed around her.

"You'd better get one," McGee warned, "because my Halloween party is on Sunday, and everyone has to be in costume or they don't get in. It says so right on the invitation."

"Who've you invited?" Zan asked, slipping her book into the tapestry bag lying by her feet.

"There are a few kids coming from my school and a couple of guys from my hockey team," McGee replied.

Each of the girls attended a different school in the city. McGee was a sixth-grader at Fairview Elementary School. She was also the only girl on the Fairview Express, the hottest hockey team in the youth league.

Then McGee added, "The rest are from the Academy."

5

Gwen, who had been quietly munching on M&Ms, nearly choked. "You didn't invite the Bunheads, did you?"

McGee looked at her hands and nodded miserably. "My mom made me."

A chorus of groans greeted her announcement.

The Bunheads were their archenemies. They were the girls in the Saturday morning ballet class who thought they were better than everyone else, and never let anyone — particularly the gang — forget it. From the moment the gang had met during a holiday production of *The Nutcracker,* the Bunheads had tried to get them kicked out of the Academy.

"You couldn't have invited them!" Rocky protested.

"It's bad enough that Courtney Clay and her snotty friends are in *Dracula* with us," Gwen added, wrinkling her nose. "But do they have to come to the party, too?"

"My mother said it would be a good chance for us to make up and become friends." McGee stuck her finger down her throat to demonstrate how she felt about her mother's idea.

"Courtney doesn't want to be our friend," Rocky declared, tucking a mass of her wild black hair behind one ear. "She just wants to make our lives miserable."

"Yeah." Gwen popped another handful of M&Ms

in her mouth. "Just because her family is rich and her mom's on the board of directors of the ballet, she thinks she's really special."

"The Bunheads at our party?" Rocky repeated with a moan. "They'll spoil everything."

"Forget about the Bunheads," McGee said. Then she leaned in and whispered, " 'Cause I also invited some very *special* people."

Gwen gave her a cautious look. "How special?"

"Special, as in really cute."

Mary Bubnik's eyes lit up and she squealed, "McGee, you didn't!"

McGee clapped her hand over Mary's mouth. "Cool it, will you?" she hissed, gesturing with her head at the door to the theatre. "*They* might hear you."

Gwen swallowed the rest of her M&Ms with a huge gulp. "Katie McGee," she said solemnly, "don't tell me you invited the boys from St. Luke's?"

McGee smiled and nodded. "Yep."

St. Luke's was a boy's school in Deerfield, and Miss Jo, one of the ballet school's directors, had been invited to teach their fifth- and sixth-grade boys in a dance appreciation class. When the production of *Dracula* had been scheduled, a number of the boys were cast as Dracula's bats, along with the gang.

"But we're too scared to talk to those boys at

7

dance rehearsal," Gwen protested. "How are we going to talk to them at a party?"

"You don't have to talk to them," McGee explained. "You can just dance with them."

"No way." Rocky leaped down onto the platform from the ladder. "I'm not dancing in front of those guys. I'd die of embarrassment."

"You're dancing in front of them now, and you're not embarrassed," McGee pointed out logically.

"That's because this is a ballet," Rocky retorted. "Mr. Anton told us to put on plastic fangs and run around in a circle waving our arms up and down like bats. We're all doing the same thing. Besides, we're in costume. We don't look as silly."

"You'll be in costume at my party," McGee said. "Wear a mask and they'll never know who you are."

"Sure." Mary Bubnik giggled. "With a mask and a costume, you could pass as the Monster of Mulberry Avenue."

Just as she finished her sentence, the music from the ballet swelled in a crescendo of trumpets, ending with a deafening crash of cymbals that made everyone jump.

Zan stuck her head inside the stage door and listened intently. "It sounds like Dracula has just had the stake driven through his heart," she called back softly to the others. "Now Lucy and Jonathan are dancing their tearful reunion." Lucy and Jonathan

8

were the names of the romantic couple in the story.

Gwen rose to her feet and dusted off her hands. "That means we'd better go to the dressing room, get our fangs, and line up for the curtain call."

The rest of the girls stood up and smoothed out their capes.

"Ready, bats?" Rocky said, holding the door open for them.

The four girls adjusted their capes and murmured, "Ready."

They trooped inside and Rocky closed the door behind them with a clang. As she did, there was a sudden blinding flash of light from the stage and the theatre was instantly cloaked in darkness.

Chapter Two

"I'm afraid," Mary Bubnik's voice moaned from the dark. "What's happening?"

She was answered by a booming male voice. "The electricity has gone off, people." It was Mr. Anton, the head of the Academy and director of the ballet. "Do not panic and *don't move* — you might hurt yourselves."

The girls stood just inside the stage door, staring into the darkness. They could hear the other dancers murmuring nervously and the sound of people shuffling across the stage.

"I don't like this," Mary Bubnik rasped. "I don't like it one bit. The lights should have come back on by now." She clutched McGee's arm so hard that her nails dug into McGee's skin.

"Cut it out, Mary," McGee cried, prying Mary's fingers off her arm. "You're giving me the heebie-jeebies."

"Take a deep breath, Mary, and try to think calm thoughts," Zan whispered. "You won't feel so frightened."

Mary inhaled loudly and, holding her breath, squeaked, "What should I think about?"

"Ice-cream sundaes with extra whipped cream," Gwen murmured from behind her. "Superdeluxe pizzas with everything on them but anchovies, and root beer floats." She hadn't eaten dinner and her stomach was starting to growl.

"That won't calm her down," Rocky muttered. "That'll give her indigestion."

Suddenly, there was a loud hum and the emergency lights above the doors backstage clicked on, casting narrow beams of greenish light around the theatre.

"Dancers, it will be another minute before we have full power," Mr. Anton shouted from the auditorium. "As soon as we do, we will start from Dracula's Dance of Death."

"That will give us just enough time to go to the dressing room and get our fangs," McGee told the others.

11

"Be careful," Mr. Anton cautioned everyone. "We don't need any broken legs this close to opening night."

One by one, dark-cloaked figures passed through the eerie pools of green light as they headed toward the stage. The only sound that the girls heard was the light padding of ballet slippers on the wooden floor and the soft whisper of costumes as the dancers moved through the wings.

"Let's take a shortcut to the costume shop and cross behind the scenery," Rocky suggested. The girls started to form a line with Rocky leading, but Mary Bubnik hung back nervously.

"But it's dark back there," she protested.

"We'll just follow the glow paint," Zan said.

"What's that?" Mary Bubnik asked.

"It's paint that holds light and turns green in the dark," Rocky explained. "They use it in the theatre all the time so the actors can see backstage. They also use glow tape." Rocky had taken several drama classes on Curtiss-Dobbs Air Force Base, where her family lived, and was the gang's expert on acting.

"See?" Zan pointed at a small, fluorescent green circle on the edge of a pillar. "There's one."

"Look for the bright green circles," Rocky instructed. She pulled back a heavy, black drape and stuck her hand out in front of her. Her hand bumped

12

into something soft. "What's this?" she asked, poking it with her finger.

Zan, who was right behind Rocky, leaned over her shoulder and felt the object with her hand. "It feels like a . . ."

"A body!" they squealed in unison.

Suddenly, a flashlight flicked on and shone in their faces.

"What are you kids doing, poking people in the stomach?" a gruff voice demanded.

"Thad?" Rocky hissed, shielding her face from the glaring light. "Is that you?"

"Well, of course, it's me. Who'd you expect to find on guard backstage?"

To prove it, the security guard shone the flashlight on his own face. Thaddeus Taylor's long face looked even more gaunt in the harsh light, and his thin, pointy nose cast a long shadow across his forehead. One eye twitched slightly as he said, "Hadn't you better get to your places? The electricity should be on any minute."

"We were following the glow tape," Rocky explained, "and we got a little confused."

Thad shone his flashlight in the other direction. "That's the way you want to go, right behind the set to the other side. I'll hold the light for you."

"Thank you, Mr. Taylor, sir," Mary Bubnik said as

they scurried toward the narrow passageway. Just as they reached it, Zan abruptly locked her knees. Mary Bubnik crashed into her back and the others followed suit.

"What's the matter now?" McGee called from the back of the line.

"I can't go back there," Zan said in a timid voice.

"Why not?"

"Because Dracula is there."

The girls inhaled sharply as they noticed a tall, thin figure dressed in a black cape and tuxedo standing behind the painted backdrop. Armand Van Valkenberg was waiting for his cue to enter the stage, the green emergency lights sculpting deep hollows in his cheeks and eyes.

"Now *he's* scary," Gwen whispered.

Mary Bubnik nodded. "He has that weird accent, and those blue eyes that look downright evil. Even his hair looks like Dracula's." The dancer's jet black hair narrowed to a point in the middle of his forehead.

"Where did they get him from?" Rocky wondered.

"He's a guest dancer from Amsterdam," Zan explained. "That's why he has that accent. The newspaper said that he's danced the role of Dracula all over the world."

"Well, he's perfect for the part," Gwen declared.

"Too perfect, if you ask me," Mary Bubnik whispered.

"Come on." McGee grabbed Mary by the hand. "We'll just run by him. We don't even have to say hello."

Mary Bubnik jerked her hand away and shrank back. "No way. He could grab us with those long arms of his and bite us on the neck."

"Mary, he's not really a vampire," Rocky said impatiently. "He's just pretending to be one."

Mary Bubnik stuck her face up close to Rocky's. "How can you be sure?"

"Why don't we go back the other way and cross under the stage?" Zan suggested.

"Good idea," McGee said. "But we'd better hurry before he sees us."

At that moment, Armand Van Valkenberg turned and saw the girls. He raised one winged arm and called, "You there. You bats."

"Too late," Gwen murmured.

McGee gulped. "Who, us?"

"What other bats are there?" He pointed to the space next to him. "Come here, please. We must talk."

"That's it," Mary moaned. "He's going to bite our necks and suck out all of our blood, and we'll be vampires forever."

"Can it, Mary!" Rocky hissed. "He might hear you."

Armand took two long strides toward them and said, "I wanted to tell you that your dance today was very good."

All five girls stared at him, openmouthed. No one ever told them they were good dancers, and to have the star of the show say it was even more astonishing.

"Really?" Mary Bubnik squeaked.

"Yes." The dancer smiled, which made him look even more ghoulish. "I know your steps are simple, but you do them very well. Keep up the good work."

"Gee, thanks, Mr. Armand," McGee finally choked out. "We think you're pretty good, too."

"Why, thank you," he said. Then the smile vanished from his face. "Now you must leave me because I must concentrate." He turned back to face the curtain, wrapping his cape around him like a cocoon. Just as he ducked his head under the hood of his cape, the lights hummed back to life. Suddenly, the stage was brightly lit and the girls blinked at each other in surprise.

"All right, everyone," Mr. Anton called from the auditorium. "We're ready to go."

Armand didn't move a muscle. He just stood like a dark statue shrouded in black.

"He must be getting into his character," Rocky whispered. "Come on, let's go."

16

The girls inched their way past the tall dancer and took the stairs to the costume and makeup room on the lower floor.

Once they were in the clear, Gwen declared matter-of-factly, "He's not so bad. In fact, he's kind of nice."

"Don't be fooled," Mary Bubnik warned. "That's how Dracula is supposed to behave. He makes everyone like him and then, when you least expect it, he bites your neck."

Rocky shot Mary a skeptical look. "Mary, I think you are seriously in danger of losing your mind."

"Yeah, what's gotten into you?" Gwen demanded. "You're not usually this wimpy about the dark."

"Oh, I know," Mary Bubnik replied sheepishly. "It's just this weird feeling I have. Kind of like permanent butterflies in your stomach. It makes me think we're about to meet something terrible."

Gwen threw open the door and there, standing at the mirror, was Courtney Clay. She was tucking a flower into the tight bun on the top of her head.

"You were right," Gwen said to Mary, "and that terrible something is the Bunheads."

Chapter Three

"What are you guys doing here?" Courtney snapped at the girls without taking her eyes off her reflection in the mirror.

Her best friends, Page Tuttle and Alice Wescott, stood beside Courtney, applying fresh coats of red lipstick. "Aren't the bats supposed to go first in the curtain call?" Alice asked in her nasal voice.

"We just stopped in to pick up our fangs," Gwen said, holding up the white plastic teeth resting on the makeup table. "What's your excuse?"

Page patted the blonde bun that perched neatly on the top of her head. "We're checking our makeup."

"As villagers, we have to look pretty," Courtney added smugly.

"You'll need more than makeup for that," Rocky cracked. "How about trying major surgery."

"Ha-ha. Very funny." Courtney blotted her lips with a tissue. "You're just mad because you have to play those ugly, old bats."

"Bats aren't ugly," a voice said from behind them. "They're pretty cool."

"Tyson!" Courtney gasped. "I didn't see you there."

Tyson Bickle was one of the boys from St. Luke's. He leaned against the doorframe with his arms crossed. His friends, Joel Port and Clint Edwards, stood just behind him. All three were wearing their bat capes. "Bats sleep upside down and can fly in the dark." Tyson flashed a smile, revealing his plastic fangs. "That's because they have radar."

"Oh, Tyson, you don't understand." Courtney giggled at the handsome blond and her face turned a bright pink. "I was talking about *them*." She waved her hand in the gang's direction. "They're the only girls at our ballet school who didn't get cast as villagers."

Tyson shrugged. "So?"

"Villagers are the prettiest and best dancers," Courtney finished.

Rocky had been clenching her jaw angrily as she

listened to Courtney insult them in front of the boys from St. Luke's. Finally, she slammed her fist on the dressing room table. "That does it. I say we knock their buns off and *then* ..." She raised her cape in the air and, baring her fangs, swooped toward Courtney with her arms outstretched. "We suck their blood!"

Courtney didn't know how to respond. First she giggled nervously, looking at Tyson and his friends to see what their reactions were. Then her expression changed to fear as Rocky grew closer.

"You stay away from me, Rocky Garcia!" Courtney cried, backing up toward the door.

"We're Dracula's bats," Rocky roared, still advancing. "We bite villagers and make them suffer."

"Tyson, stop her!" Courtney leaped behind the muscular boy, who chuckled and asked, "How?"

"I don't know," Courtney whined. "Just make her stop. She's a big bully."

Rocky dropped her cape in disgust. "And you, Courtney Clay, are a big wimp."

Courtney didn't respond to Rocky's remark. She clutched Tyson's arm and cooed, "Thanks, Ty. You really protected me."

Rocky rolled her eyes at the gang. "Come on. Let's get out of here before I throw up."

She started to lead the others toward the door but

Courtney blocked their way. Still clinging to Tyson's arm, she said, "I hope you're coming to my party next Sunday, Tyson."

"Party!" McGee gasped. "What party?"

Courtney ignored her. "Did you and your friends get my invitation?"

"Uh, yeah," the boy replied, drawing a circle on the floor with the toe of his ballet shoe.

"Are you coming?" Courtney repeated.

Tyson looked sheepishly at McGee through the lock of hair that had fallen over one eye. "I'm not sure. I'll, uh . . . let you know later."

Before either girl could say another word, Tyson had grabbed his buddies and run out the doorway. McGee waited until they were out of sight and then hissed, "You can't have your party on Sunday. That's when I'm having mine."

"So?" Courtney shrugged.

"My mom already okayed the food and all the activities and everything," McGee explained. "I sent out the invitations last week."

Courtney pretended to yawn. "Gee, that's too bad. I guess you'll just have to cancel."

"She's not canceling," Gwen barked. "She had the idea first."

"So I had it second," Courtney retorted. "But mine will be better."

McGee clenched her teeth in frustration. "Court-ney Clay, if you throw a party on Sunday, I'm not coming."

"You're not invited." Courtney folded her arms across her chest. "Only the *good* dancers at the Academy are coming." She smiled innocently. "And, of course, all the boys from St. Luke's."

"But they're already invited to my party!" McGee protested.

Courtney turned and casually checked her makeup in the mirror one last time. "Want to bet on whose party they go to?"

Rocky stepped forward. "Sure. What's the bet?"

Courtney put one finger to her chin and tilted her head in thought. Finally, she said, "If I win and the boys come to my party, then all five of you will leave the Deerfield Academy of Dance forever."

"It's a deal," Rocky said quickly.

McGee's eyes widened. "Rocky, now wait a min-ute . . ."

"What's the matter, McGee, afraid that you'll lose?" Page Tuttle taunted from in front of the mirror.

McGee spun around angrily. "No, I'm not. My party will be much more fun than Courtney's."

Gwen asked, "But what do they have to do if we win?"

"Same thing," Rocky said firmly.

"I'm sorry, but I just can't agree to that," Courtney

22

said. "You see, my mother is on the board of directors and she would never allow me to leave the Academy."

"Something else then." Rocky motioned the gang into a huddle. "Okay," she whispered, "let's make her do something really disgusting, like eat live worms."

"That's really gross." Mary Bubnik wrinkled her nose. "I think we should make her do something for us."

"Let's make Courtney bring us pizzas and milk shakes after every ballet class for the rest of the year." Gwen smiled wickedly. "She could be our personal slave."

"But then we'd have to see her all the time," McGee pointed out. "And that would be punishing *us*."

"I've got it." Zan snapped her fingers. "The Bunheads think they're so much better than us, right?"

They all nodded.

"Then we'll make her cancel her party and come to McGee's, where she will make a formal announcement to the entire group that *we* are the best dancers in our class."

"That's the best idea yet," McGee cried gleefully. "It'll kill her."

"She'd never be able to do it," Gwen said, shaking her head.

23

Rocky set her jaw firmly. "She'll have to if she wants to keep this bet."

Courtney's face paled for just a second when Rocky told her their side of the bet. Finally, she said, "I'll agree to that *only* because I know I'm going to win."

Suddenly, the intercom speaker crackled above their heads. "Dracula's bats? Come to the stage this instant," a voice shouted. "You're late for the curtain call."

"Now you're in trouble with Mr. Anton," Courtney jeered. "Nice going."

Rocky started to raise her fist at Courtney but McGee hurriedly grabbed her arm. "Not now. We've got to get on stage."

The girls bolted out of the dressing room and raced down the hall to the stairs that led to the stage. As they stepped into the wings, the stage manager announced over the headset, "The bats are here. We can start the call."

"It's about time," Mr. Anton shouted from the audience. "Now, quickly, people, let's get through this thing so we can rehearse the specialty numbers once more. It's going to be a long evening."

The conductor raised his baton and the curtain call music began. Rocky led the girls onto the stage, performing the movements that they had been rehearsing for the past six weeks. They raised their

24

capes and ran to the center of the stage. As the tallest, Zan was positioned in the middle, and she whispered, "Bow." The others nodded their heads, curtsied, then quickly backed up to form a line along the piece of scenery that was painted to look like a castle.

As the music continued, the boys from St. Luke's ran on to take their bows, followed by group after group of dancers. Soon the stage was filled with bats and villagers. When the principal dancers came on, the music swelled. McGee whispered out of the corner of her mouth, "I'm really worried, you guys."

"Don't sweat it," Rocky whispered back. "Mr. Anton will just give us one of his icy stares, and maybe yell at us for being late, but it'll only be embarrassing for a minute."

"I'm not worried about that," McGee replied. "I'm worried about my party. How are we going to get the boys from St. Luke's to come?"

"There's no need to panic," Mary Bubnik said. "We've got four whole days to come up with a plan."

"It'd better be a good one," Gwen warned. "Or else our dancing days are over."

Chapter Four

The next evening before rehearsal, the girls met for dinner at their favorite hangout — Hi Lo's Pizza and Chinese Food To Go. The little restaurant was tucked in between a loan office and a jewelry store, and the red-and-white awning over its door rippled in the chilly breeze. Rocky threw open the door, and a little brass bell above their heads signaled their arrival.

A slender, old Chinese man was leaning against the circular lunch counter, a pair of silver wire-rimmed glasses perched on the end of his nose. No one else was in the tiny restaurant, which only had a few stools along the counter and two booths in the back. Hi Lo was absorbed in his newspaper but at the sound of the bell, he looked up. His face crinkled into a warm smile when he recognized the gang.

"My favorite ballerinas have arrived," he declared. "What a pleasant surprise!"

"Hi, Hi!" Gwen shouted as she hopped onto one of the worn, red leather stools. "We need food, and we need it fast!"

Hi folded his newspaper and tucked it under the counter. "Then you've come to the right place. But what's your rush?"

Mary Bubnik took the stool next to Gwen and explained, "We're rehearsing the Academy's new ballet, *Dracula*. It's going to be a big hit. It's really scary, and you should see the guy playing Dracula. His name is Armand and he's practically a giant."

Gwen cleared her throat. "Mary, get to the point."

"The point?" Mary Bubnik blinked her big blue eyes at Gwen. "Oh, yeah. You see, we only have a short time to eat dinner and come up with a plan."

"Plan?" Hi interrupted. "What sort of plan?"

"Let me tell it." Rocky leaned forward with her hands on the counter. "It's like this — we made a bet with the Bunheads that we could get the boys from St. Luke's to come to McGee's Halloween party, and not theirs."

"Who are the boys from St. Luke's?" Hi cut in.

"Just the coolest guys to ever set foot in Deer-

27

field," McGee replied, flipping up the brim of her baseball cap.

"Oh." He nodded wisely. "*Those* boys from St. Luke's."

"You see," Mary Bubnik said, "if they don't come to McGee's party, then we'll have to quit the Academy."

"And that would truly be a disaster," Zan added. "We'd never see each other or you again."

Hi stroked his chin. "That *is* a problem. And it calls for a *special* Hi Lo Special." He pointed to the special written on the blackboard above the milkshake mixer: "Chop Suey Surprise."

"Surprise?" Gwen repeated. "What kind of surprise could be in chop suey?"

"If I told you, then it wouldn't be a surprise." Hi slipped an apron over his head. He paused at the swinging door into the kitchen and said, "Trust me. It's delicious, nutritious, and just the thing for hungry dancers like you." As the door swung shut behind him, they heard him giggling.

Gwen arched an eyebrow. "I think Hi has been watching too much television. He sounds just like a commercial."

"You don't think he'd put one of his secret ingredients in the chop suey?" Mary Bubnik asked warily. Hi was famous for his secret ingredients. Usually he added them to milk shakes, and occasionally to pizza. "I mean, peanut butter was fine in a chocolate shake, but I think it would taste kind of weird in Chinese food."

"Weird?" Rocky grimaced. "It would taste awful."

"Forget about the secret ingredient," McGee said, nervously chewing on her fingernails. "We need to concentrate on a plan to make my party a hit. I had nightmares all last night worrying about it."

Zan pulled her lavender pad and her favorite pen out of her tapestry bag. "Let's make a list of things we'll need for the party."

"Food," Gwen said matter-of-factly. "Put that at the top of the list."

"What kind of food?" Zan asked.

"I think chips and unusual dips are always a plus at any party," Gwen declared. "My mother says finger foods really get the guests involved." Mrs. Hays was an expert on entertaining and considered herself the perfect hostess.

"I think having fun games is more important," McGee said. "Maybe we could play Red Rover and Dodge Ball —"

"And Spin the Bottle," Mary added with a mischievous giggle.

"What's that?" Rocky asked.

All four girls gaped at her in surprise.

"I thought everybody knew about Spin the Bottle," Gwen said.

"Well, I'm not everybody," Rocky replied, crossing her arms over her chest. "Tell me what it is."

The girls looked at each other, giggling with embarrassment, until finally Mary Bubnik blurted out, "You put a pop bottle on the floor and everyone sits in a circle around it. Then someone spins it — "

"Like one of the boys from St. Luke's," Zan explained.

"Right," Mary Bubnik nodded at Zan, "and whichever girl it points to when it stops, he has to kiss."

"Kiss!" Rocky stumbled backward off her stool. "No way. I'm not kissing any guy." She put her hands on her hips and shot them a fierce glare. "If this party is going to include kissing, then you can count me out."

"Rocky, calm down," McGee said. "Mary was just joking."

Before Rocky could reply, the kitchen door swung open and Hi stood in the entrance, carrying a big, round, silver platter. On the tray were five bowls of rice covered with what looked like gooey chicken stew. "Dinner is served!"

Hi set a bowl in front of each girl, along with a fork and a napkin. The girls stared down at the mixture and back up at Mr. Lo. He grinned broadly and, with a flick of his wrist, said, "Dig in. It's good."

Gwen was so ravenous that she didn't need any

encouragement. She scooped up a large portion of the chop suey and crammed it into her mouth.

The others hesitated, their forks suspended above their bowls. Finally, Zan asked, "Did you put one of your famous secret ingredients in it?"

Hi nodded proudly. "I most certainly did."

"What is it?" Mary Bubnik asked.

Gwen stopped chewing in mid-bite. Her eyes widened and she choked out, "Bananas."

"Right you are," Hi said. "Fried bananas."

"Oh, gross!" Rocky pushed her bowl away from her in disgust.

"Now, wait a minute," Hi protested. "I think you should at least try it before you reject it." He winked at Gwen encouragingly. "It's good, isn't it, Gwen?"

Gwen swallowed hard. "Well, it certainly is *different,*" she said tactfully.

Before any of the others could try Hi's concoction for themselves, the door to the restaurant burst open and an elderly woman carrying several shopping bags stumbled into the room. "Call the police!" she gasped. "I've been booed!"

Hi rushed to the lady's side and helped her to one of the two booths lining the rear of the tiny restaurant. Mary Bubnik scooted behind the counter and quickly poured a glass of water, while the rest of the girls huddled in a circle around the distraught woman.

"Did someone hurt you?" Hi asked as he took the glass of water from Mary and offered it to the woman.

She took a large gulp, then shook her head. "I was leaving Baumgartner's department store and as I passed the alley on Mulberry Avenue, some...
thing leaped out at me."

Rocky turned to the girls and whispered, "The Monster of Mulberry Avenue."

The short, pudgy woman was wearing a red wool coat with a plaid scarf tied around her head. Her face was flushed so red that it matched her coat. "He must have been ten feet tall and had a hideous skeleton face," she continued in a shaking voice. "He raised his arms and then, in this eerie voice, cried, 'Boo!'"

"What did you do?" McGee asked.

"I-I don't really know." The woman grabbed one of the paper napkins from the metal dispenser on the table and dabbed at the perspiration dotting her face. "I threw my arms in the air and ran. I think I might have dropped my purse." She patted her pockets, and then frantically clawed through her shopping bags. "Oh, dear, I did drop it. I'd better go back for it."

"It won't be there," Rocky whispered in McGee's ear. "That's how he gets people's money. He scares them, they drop their purses, and then he accidentally-on-purpose finds them."

32

The woman was struggling to get up when McGee pressed her hand against the lady's arm. "You stay here, Ms., uh . . ."

"Dinwiddie," the woman said. "Estelle Dinwiddie."

"Ms. Dinwiddie," McGee repeated. "We'll go look for your purse."

"Thank you, honey." Ms. Dinwiddie sank back into the booth with a sigh of relief. "Frankly, I don't think I've got the strength."

"You just sit there until you feel rested," Hi agreed, patting the old woman on the shoulder. "I'll fix you a hot cup of tea."

"But what about ballet rehearsal?" Mary Bubnik whispered as Hi and the girls headed back toward the counter. "We're supposed to be at the auditorium in fifteen minutes."

"We can look for her purse on the way," Zan said, slipping her lavender pad into her tapestry bag. "Then we'll call Hi from the theatre."

"Good thinking," Hi said, moving behind the counter. "In the meantime, I'll call the police."

"Come on," Zan said, slipping her purple beret on her head and pulling on her trench coat. "We want to get there first and look for clues."

"Clues?" Rocky paused, putting one arm through the sleeve of her embroidered red satin jacket.

"Uh-oh," Gwen muttered. "Zan's got that Tiffany Truenote, Teen Detective look in her eye."

33

"What's that mean?" Mary Bubnik asked, as she zipped up her pink parka.

McGee tossed her scarf over her shoulder. "It means we're going hunting for the Monster of Mulberry Avenue."

Chapter Five

Zan led the girls down Main Street to Mulberry Avenue. She could hardly contain her excitement. She was going to get the chance to discover who was scaring the citizens of Deerfield. Just like Tiffany Truenote, she would save the city and become a hero. She might even get her picture in the newspaper.

"We're too late," Rocky shouted as they rounded the corner onto Mulberry Avenue. "The cops are already there."

A patrol car was double-parked at the entrance to the alley, its flashers casting red shadows around the buildings and street. A policeman standing by the entrance to Baumgartner's was surrounded by a small crowd of people.

"How did they get there so fast?" McGee said. "Hi just called the police."

"I believe this policeman must have responded to a separate cry for help," Zan said in the tight, clipped voice she liked to use when she was discussing a case.

"How can you tell?" Mary Bubnik asked.

"The two ladies closest to him resemble the victim we just saw at Hi Lo's," Zan replied. "They're both elderly, they both have more than two shopping bags, and they are both missing the same thing."

"What's that?" McGee asked.

"A purse." Zan was busily making notes as she spoke. "It would be my guess that they are also victims of the Monster of Mulberry Avenue."

"Let's go closer and see if you're right." Rocky shoved her way through the crowd to the policeman's side. The rest of the gang was on her heels.

"He was huge, with long, long arms!" an old lady with stringy gray hair was exclaiming to the officer. "He had a horrible face like a skull! Then he leaped out of the alley at me and shouted, 'Boo!' "

"Boo?" The policeman paused in writing down her story and stared at her for a moment. "That's all?"

"That was enough." The woman tugged at her

36

coat indignantly. "He scared the living daylights out of me."

The officer pushed his hat back on his head. "So what did you do?"

"I threw my purse at him."

"That was smart," the officer said with a smirk. "And then what happened?"

"He must have taken it because it's gone and I'm out fifty dollars." The woman shook her head and moaned, "Milton is going to kill me."

The policeman perked up at this information. "Who's Milton?"

"My husband."

The other old lady tugged at the policeman's sleeve. "That's exactly what happened to me."

"Boy," Zan murmured to the others, "the Monster is really active tonight."

"Let's get to the theatre, you guys," Mary Bubnik said, anxiously looking over her shoulder into the dark recesses of the buildings across the street. "I'm really scared."

The girls watched as the officer helped the two older women into his patrol car. "I can't get over it," Gwen said suddenly. "It's incredible."

"What?" Zan asked, thinking Gwen had heard some new bit of information about the Monster from the people in the crowd.

Gwen pointed to the parcels the old ladies were

37

carrying. "Look at the size of Baumgartner's shopping bags. They're huge."

"So?" Rocky said.

"So they'd make the perfect trick-or-treat bag for Halloween," Gwen replied. "I bet those things could hold a ton of candy."

"Gwen!" Rocky put her hands on her hips and glared at her friend. "Three people have just been booed, for crying out loud, and all you can think about is trick-or-treating?"

"It's important," Gwen said, as the girls crossed the street and made their way to the civic auditorium. "Halloween only comes once a year. Having the right trick-or-treat bag can make a big difference."

"How?"

"Well, if the bag is too flimsy, it might break and you'll lose all your candy. If it's too small, people will only drop one thing in it — a stick of gum, or one of those little snack cakes. It needs to be just large enough that people will give you two handfuls, but not so big that you look greedy."

Rocky stared at her friend, dumbfounded. "You've really been thinking about this, haven't you?"

"Of course." Gwen removed her glasses and polished them carefully on the trim of her pink down jacket. "I don't know about you, but I take trick-or-treating very seriously. If you do it right, it can mean a three-month supply of candy." She placed her glasses back onto her nose and smiled. "Think about it."

Suddenly, a bloodcurdling scream pierced the air. McGee spun and pointed behind her. "That cry came from the alley behind Polar Bear Ice Cream."

"What are we waiting for?" Zan said. "Come on!"

"Don't we have to get to rehearsal?" Mary Bubnik asked, pointing the other way.

Zan hopped off the curb into the street. "And miss out on a chance of seeing the Monster of Mulberry Avenue?"

"No way!" Rocky cried. She and McGee raced after Zan.

Mary and Gwen shrugged at each other and shuffled after the others, who had charged across the street, and ran headlong into the Bunheads.

"Aren't you going in the wrong direction?" Courtney asked. "The theatre is that way," she added, pointing over Zan's shoulder.

"We can't stop to talk," Zan cried. "We've got to catch the Monster!"

"Of Mulberry Avenue?" Alice Wescott's eyes bugged out of her face with fear.

"Yeah, didn't you hear the scream? He just booed two ladies outside of Baumgartner's," McGee explained. "And now he's gotten someone else behind Polar Bear Ice Cream."

Zan dug in her pocket for the flashlight that was

39

part of her official Tiffany Truenote detective kit. She aimed it at the alley and the narrow beam was swallowed up by the darkness. "Come *on*. The Monster's probably still in there. Let's go find him."

"If you don't mind," Mary Bubnik said timidly, "I'll just stay here with the Bun — I mean, Courtney and her friends."

"Don't you want to see what the Monster looks like?" Zan asked in astonishment.

"You can tell us about it," Gwen said, linking arms with Mary Bubnik. "I'm going to keep Mary company."

Zan turned to Rocky and McGee, who both looked a little pale. "What about you guys?"

"Um, I've been thinking about it, Zan," McGee said, carefully eyeing the dark alley. "What if we actually do run into the Monster? What should we do?"

"Capture him, of course."

"With what?" Rocky asked.

"With whatever's around," Zan replied. "In the last book, Tiffany used a garbage can she found in an alley. She dropped it over the crook's head and pinned his arms to his sides. He stayed that way until the police came." She tried to control her impatience. "Don't you remember? I read it to you just last week."

"But that was a book, Zan," Rocky pointed out. "This is real life."

"What's the matter, Rochelle?" Courtney taunted. "Chicken?"

"Of course not," Rocky snapped, her nostrils flaring with anger. "I'm just being careful. We'll see you dweebs later." She zipped up her satin jacket and stepped into the alley. Zan turned to the others, who shrugged and reluctantly followed her.

"Stay in the middle of the alley," Zan whispered. "The Monster could be hiding in any one of the doorways, just waiting to grab us."

"Just what we needed to hear," Rocky grumbled.

As they tiptoed along the pavement, Mary Bubnik moaned, "The butterflies in my stomach are really going to town again. I don't like this. I don't like it at all."

"Geez Louise, Mary," McGee muttered, "can't you put a lid on that?"

After they'd gone just a few feet, Gwen looked over her shoulder and ordered, "Stop."

"What for?" Mary Bubnik clutched Gwen's arm in fear. "Do you see him?"

Gwen shook her head. "The Bunheads are gone. We can go back now."

"What do you mean, go back?" Rocky demanded. "Aren't we going to find the Monster?"

"Definitely not," Gwen replied. "That's something for the police to do, not a bunch of fifth- and sixth-graders."

41

"Then why did you come along?" McGee asked.

"I didn't want the Bunheads to think we were scaredy-cats," Gwen explained. "But now that they've gone to the theatre we can just *pretend* we went after him. They'll never know the difference."

"It doesn't matter, anyway," Zan said, kneeling down to examine the street. "The Monster's already gone."

"How do you know?" Mary asked.

Zan shone her flashlight along the muddy alley. "See how the gravel's all churned up here? It looks like there was some kind of scuffle."

"I'm sorry we missed him," Rocky said, patting Zan on the shoulder.

"That's truly all right," Zan replied, "because I've found another clue to add to my list."

The gang stared down at the muddy pavement. None of them could see anything but a couple of mud puddles and some torn pieces of a shopping bag. McGee looked up with a puzzled expression on her face. "What clue?"

"Right here." Zan pointed to a long, narrow depression in the mud. "This footprint." She pulled a small tape measure out of her tapestry bag and stretched it the length of the print. "I'd say that our Monster has about a size-twelve foot."

"Well, of course he has a size twelve," Gwen said.

42

"At seven feet tall, he should have at least a size fifteen."

"My point, exactly." Zan folded up the tape measure with a crisp snap. "Maybe our Monster isn't really seven feet tall at all. Maybe he's just disguised to *look* taller."

"How?" Rocky asked.

Zan tapped her pen on her lips. "I'll have to think about this some more." She rose to her feet and faced the others. "In the meantime, we bats had better get to the theatre."

"Or Mr. Anton will make us unemployed bats," Gwen cracked.

The girls flew like the wind down the street toward the theatre, partly because they didn't want to be late, but mostly because they wanted to get away from the Monster of Mulberry Avenue.

Chapter Six

"Well, here come the great detectives," Page Tuttle declared as McGee and the gang ran down the hall of the theatre to their dressing rooms. She and Alice Wescott were standing with Courtney Clay, talking to the boys from St. Luke's.

Tyson looked confused and Courtney explained, "They were after the Monster of Mulberry Avenue."

"That guy who's been booing old ladies?" he asked.

Zan nodded. "He booed three more victims just on our dinner break. We happened to be right at the scene of the crime."

"Weren't you scared?" Joel asked, looking very impressed. "I hear that guy's seven feet tall."

"Zan has a theory about—" McGee started to say, but Courtney cut her off.

"I'm sure the boys don't want to hear your silly theories," Courtney snapped. "Before I was so rudely interrupted, I was telling Ty and his friends about my exciting visit to the caterers. Mother and I had a private interview with Phillipe to discuss all the arrangements for my party."

"Caterers?" McGee muttered. "What are they?"

Courtney rolled her eyes. "Every *good* party has a caterer. They prepare your food and then serve it for you personally." She smiled sweetly at Ty and added, "We'll be having eight different kinds of club sandwiches, cocktail sausages, cheese and chocolate fondue, and a big Waldorf salad. And for dessert, Phillipe himself is going to bake a huge devil's food cake in the shape of a pumpkin, with ice-cream filling, and little marzipan witches and goblins on the icing."

Tyson and the boys exchanged uncertain looks. "Gee, sounds pretty fancy."

"Oh, it's just a little get-together among friends," Courtney replied, lightly patting her bun. "But my mother always says, if you're going to do something, do it right."

"So what are you having at your party, McGee?" Page asked with a taunting smile.

"I, uh, er, I hadn't really thought about it...," McGee stammered. The question had caught her by surprise. "I figured we'd have some chips and dips, you know, pizza, stuff like that."

"*Bor*-ing!" Courtney said, making a big show of stifling a yawn with her hand. "But maybe you can salvage things with your choice of entertainment."

"Oh, we've got that all worked out," Mary Bubnik replied confidently. "We're playing games."

"Games?" Courtney laughed out loud. "How quaint."

"Nobody plays games anymore," Page whispered loudly to Alice Wescott, who giggled.

"My mother has hired the best magician in Deerfield," Courtney informed the boys.

"Just for your party?" Joel exclaimed. "Hey, that's cool!"

"I thought you'd like it," Courtney purred. "Why, he's even going to saw me in half."

"Permanently?" Gwen asked hopefully.

"Of course not."

Gwen snapped her fingers. "Too bad."

Courtney turned her back on the gang and added, "Then he's going to teach us all a few magic tricks."

"Gee, Courtney, that sounds pretty fantastic," McGee murmured. She was starting to get very depressed. What had ever given her the idea she could throw a party? She hadn't even known what a caterer was.

"So have you and the other boys from St. Luke's decided which Halloween party you're going to?" Courtney asked Tyson. She had the triumphant smile of a winner plastered across her face.

McGee hung her head and turned away. She didn't need to hear anymore. She already knew the answer.

"Actually, Courtney, we haven't really talked about it," Tyson said carefully. "Both parties sound real nice." Then he grinned at McGee and the gang. "You guys capture the Monster of Mulberry Avenue, and we'll be at your place for sure."

"Capture the Monster?" Joel slapped Tyson on the back and chortled, "Boy, that's a good one, Ty."

The loudspeaker crackled above their heads. The voice of the stage manager announced, "Places, please. Places for the start of the ballet."

"Uh, listen, we gotta go," Tyson said, backing out of the room. "We'll talk to you later."

After the boys left, Page Tuttle turned to Courtney and declared, "I think Tyson has a crush on you."

"Really." The way Courtney said it, the word sounded like a fact.

"Oh, of course, Courtney," Alice chimed in. "Especially in your costume. You look so beautiful!"

Courtney smiled at her reflection. "I do, don't I?"

47

"I think I'm going to be sick," Gwen said, clutching her stomach.

"Clint's awfully cute, don't you think?" Page said, sticking another bobby pin into the flower crown encircling her bun. Then she giggled and added, "I hope there'll be dancing at your party."

"Of course there will be," Courtney replied, sneaking a sideward glance to catch the gang's reaction. "Mother was even thinking about hiring a band."

Alice peeked out the door of the makeup room. "The overture is almost over, and the villagers are first on the stage. We'd better hurry."

Courtney gave her reflection one last satisfied smile, then flounced past the gang out the door.

"This is terrible," McGee groaned. She slumped down in her chair, shaking her head in misery. "Why did I have to send out invitations to my party? It's going to be a disaster. No one is going to come."

"Oh, cheer up, McGee," Mary Bubnik said brightly. "It's not that bad."

"Not that bad?" McGee crossed her eyes in disbelief. "The boys from St. Luke's won't be coming. We're going to lose the bet with Courtney. We'll have to drop out of the Academy, and then we'll probably never see each other again."

"Tyson did say they were still thinking about it," Zan pointed out.

"He's just being nice," McGee muttered. "Who in their right mind *wouldn't* want to go to a party like Courtney's?"

"Aw, snap out of it," Gwen said. "Maybe the boys from St. Luke's think Courtney's a Bunhead, just like we do."

"Fat chance," McGee mumbled.

"I've got an idea," Rocky said suddenly.

"What?"

"Remember when Tyson said, 'You capture the Monster of Mulberry Avenue, and I'll come to your party'?"

"Yeah." McGee shrugged. "But he was just joking."

"I know," Rocky replied, "but what if we actually *did* catch the Monster?" Her eyes gleamed with triumph. "Then he'd *have* to come."

"But you're talking about the impossible," Gwen said.

"Maybe not." Zan tapped her bag that she had looped over her shoulder. "I've got my list of clues."

"So do the police."

"That policeman didn't seem too keen on solving the case," Zan observed.

"But once we catch him, what do we do with him?" Mary Bubnik asked logically. "Assuming that you really can catch him."

"We, uh . . . tie him up," Rocky said.

Gwen rolled her eyes. "Yeah, sure, a seven-foot giant . . ."

Rocky ignored Gwen's remark. "We call the police and then take our picture with him to prove we caught him."

"When are we going to perform this miracle?" Gwen asked.

Zan pursed her lips. "How about tomorrow night? The principal dancers are rehearsing all day and we don't have a rehearsal."

Rocky clapped her hands together. "Then it's on."

Gwen pushed her glasses up on her nose with one pudgy finger. "It'll never work."

"It might," Zan said, rubbing her chin thoughtfully. "With a little planning."

"And a lot of luck," McGee added, perking up for the first time. "After all, what have we got to lose?"

Gwen started to reply, but Rocky said quickly, "Don't answer that."

Chapter Seven

On Thursday evening Rocky, McGee, and Mary Bubnik gathered in the alley two blocks from Baumgartner's and waited for the sun to set. Each of them
carried a shopping bag and a flashlight.

Finally Zan hurried into the alley, her trench coat
belted tightly against the evening chill. "Sorry I'm
late," she said, dropping her tapestry bag onto the
ground. "Did you bring what I told you?"

Mary Bubnik nodded. "Yeah, but it was hard." She
held up a thick coil of stout rope. "I was trying to
sneak this out of the house, but my mother caught
me and asked what I intended to do with it."

"What did you tell her?" McGee asked.

51

"I said we were planning to capture the Monster of Mulberry Avenue and tie him up."

"You told her the truth?" Rocky gasped.

Mary Bubnik nodded so hard, her curls bounced. "Y'all should have seen her laugh. She doubled over like she was about to die, and tears just poured out of her eyes."

"Boy, that burns me up," Rocky said. "Everybody thinks it's just a big joke."

"It's lucky for us that they do," Zan said. "Otherwise, our parents would never let us out of the house." She consulted the list she'd written out on her lavender pad. "Okay, we have the rope for tying him up. McGee, did you bring the binoculars?"

McGee nodded, and then held up a shiny coin. "And a quarter to dial the police."

"But you don't need to put money in a pay phone to call 911," Mary Bubnik pointed out.

"That's what they say," McGee retorted. "But it never hurts to be prepared."

"Good thinking," Rocky said, clapping McGee on the back.

Zan consulted her list again. "I brought the Polaroid." She dug in her bag and held up the instant camera by its wrist strap. "And it's got a fresh new pack of film."

"Great," Rocky said. "And I brought the decoy."

She put her fingers to her lips and whistled sharply. "Come on out!"

A tiny voice sounded from behind the big, green Dumpster near the back of the alley. "No way. Someone might see me like this."

"That's the idea." Rocky stepped behind the Dumpster and the others heard her say, "Don't worry. No one would ever recognize you."

"I still don't understand why I had to be the decoy," Gwen's voice grumbled.

"Because you have those wire-rimmed glasses, which make you look the oldest," Rocky explained, stepping back into view. "Now, come on out, the sun's almost down."

A few moments later, what appeared to be a short, plump old lady stepped into the alley.

"Wow," McGee breathed in admiration. "What a disguise!"

Gwen had borrowed her grandmother's short, black-and-white-checked wool coat, along with a pair of her mother's black pumps. A dowdy, felt hat sat on top of a gray wig Rocky had found at the thrift store. An old, black leather purse dangled from one of her arms.

"You look perfect!" Mary Bubnik cried.

"I feel ridiculous." Gwen tugged at the waistband. "I don't see why I had to wear these support hose. I feel like I'm in an all-over girdle."

"The stockings make the picture perfect," Rocky said authoritatively. "All little old ladies wear them."

"That's not true," McGee said. "My grandmother wouldn't be caught dead in these things."

Rocky was unperturbed. "Well, let's just say the little old ladies the Monster has been booing wear them."

Mary Bubnik looked closely at Gwen and examined her face carefully. "Boy, Rocky, you did a terrific job with the makeup."

"Thanks." Rocky beamed with satisfaction. "I learned how to do that in my drama class on the base." She pointed her flashlight at the tiny wrinkles drawn around Gwen's eyes. "Lots of people would just draw on lines with a black eyebrow pencil, but we were told that you're supposed to use colors that match the person's face. Then you blend them in so there aren't any sharp lines."

Gwen shooed them off with her purse. "Will you guys stop it? I feel like a bug under a microscope." She jerked her mouth from side to side. "And my face is starting to itch."

"Don't scratch it," Rocky warned. "Or you'll smear the makeup."

"Great. Wonderful." Gwen puffed out her cheeks in frustration. "Now I'm stuck like this."

"It won't be for long," Zan said, glancing up at the sky. The last light of day had faded and the alley had grown quite dark. Zan tucked her list in her pocket and, taking the shopping bags from the girls, pressed them into Gwen's arms. "We'd better get ready to set our trap for the Monster of Mulberry Avenue, or we're going to miss him." Then she pushed Gwen toward the edge of the alley. "Remember, look helpless and confused."

"I *feel* helpless and confused. And hungry!" Gwen snapped back. "Now tell me once again how I won't get hurt at all."

"I told you, the Monster never touches his victims," Zan said. "He just leaps out of an alley and yells 'boo.' When the victim drops her purse, he grabs it and runs."

"That's where we come in," Rocky said, holding up Mary Bubnik's rope. "When you drop the purse, we'll lasso him as he bends over to pick it up."

"Go stand in front of Baumgartner's." Zan pointed to the department store two blocks away. "Then, after a few minutes, stroll to the far corner past those two alleys."

"Just keep doing that until he jumps out at you," Rocky added.

"He'd better jump quick," Gwen grumbled, "'cause I'm starting to get *really* hungry. Rocky wouldn't let me eat anything with this makeup on."

"You do this," Rocky said encouragingly, "and I'll buy you a hot dog."

"A hot dog?" Gwen repeated, rolling her eyes. "Big wow."

"Hurry up and get out there," McGee said as she gently pushed Gwen out of the alley. "We'll be right behind you."

Gwen stumbled down the sidewalk, nearly dropping her shopping bags with every step. They could hear her muttering in a low voice as she tugged at her support hose. "You owe me a favor for this. A big favor. Bigger than a hot dog."

Gwen took her place in front of a window with Baumgartner's big Halloween display and stood staring miserably into the street.

"Zan?" Mary Bubnik whispered, after the girls had watched Gwen for several minutes.

"Yes?"

"Do you really think this is a good idea? What if the Monster discovers that Gwen is just a short sixth-grader in a gray wig and support hose and he gets really mad?"

"Don't worry, she'll be okay," Rocky said, clenching her fists. "We'll be right there to let him have it."

McGee, who had kept her binoculars trained on Gwen, announced, "The decoy is on the move, heading for the corner of Main and Mulberry."

Zan flipped up the collar of her trench coat. "Let's tail her."

"Hold it," McGee said, sticking out her arm to block their way. "The decoy has been waylaid."

"By who?" Zan cried.

"It looks like . . ." Suddenly McGee lowered her binoculars. "I don't believe it."

"What?" they gasped.

McGee raised the glasses to her eyes once more. "She's been surrounded by a bunch of Cub Scouts."

"Cub Scouts!" Rocky grabbed the binoculars from McGee. "Let me see."

"What are they doing out on a night like this?" Mary Bubnik asked. "It's way past their bedtime."

"They're trying to help Gwen cross the street," Rocky reported. "But she's not letting them. She's putting up quite a fight."

"We've got to stop her!" Zan cried. She ran out of the alley down the street, toward the corner where a small crowd was gathering. McGee and the others hurried after her.

"Get your hands off me," Gwen bellowed, jerking her elbow out of the Scout leader's grasp.

"But we just want to help you cross the street, ma'am," the boy said.

"Maybe I don't feel like crossing the street," Gwen retorted. "Did you ever think about that?"

"I'm sorry," he said doggedly, "but you seemed to be having trouble with your bags."

"The only trouble I'm having is with you," Gwen snapped. "Now beat it, will you?"

Gwen's loud protests and the growing crowd caught the attention of the security policeman inside Baumgartner's, who came running through the doors.

"What seems to be the problem, ma'am?" he asked politely.

"Will everyone quit calling me ma'am?" Gwen shrieked. "I'm just a kid." To prove her point, she whipped off her wig and waved it in the air. "See?"

The guard's whole attitude changed. "What's the idea of frightening people and stopping traffic?" he barked. "Halloween isn't until next week." He shooed her down the street with a wave of his hands. "Now you get on home before you cause any more trouble."

"Maybe I will!" Gwen shouted. She threw her bags at the guard and raced down the street.

"Uh-oh," McGee muttered. "She's pretty angry."

Zan nodded. "We'd better follow her and make sure she's okay."

"Do you think she's going home?" Mary Bubnik asked.

"Are you kidding?" Rocky replied. "Gwen's upset. So what does she always do when she gets mad?"

"Eat!" all four answered at once.

58

"Right." Rocky rubbed her chin thoughtfully. "My guess is that she's about to order a superthick chocolate shake, a bacon-cheeseburger, and a double order of fries."

"At Hi Lo's?" Mary Bubnik asked.

Rocky broke into a big grin. "Where else?"

Chapter Eight

When the girls reached Hi Lo's restaurant, Mary Bubnik pressed her face against the plate glass window and peered inside. "She's not at the counter, y'all!"

"That's because she's sitting in the booth in the back," McGee said, looking through the door.

"Boy, she must really be mad," Rocky said.

Zan put her hand on the door. "Let's go in. We'll sit at the counter and give her time to calm down. Then we can talk to her."

McGee nodded. "Good idea."

"Hi, Hi!" Mary Bubnik called cheerily as the girls entered the tiny restaurant. She looked over at Gwen, who didn't even raise her head. Gwen just kept staring down at the little blue menu resting on the table in front of her.

Hi stuck his head through the tiny window from the kitchen and waved at the girls. "If it isn't the rest of the five musketeers. I was wondering what happened to you." He gestured at the counter and added, "Have a seat. I'll be right out."

McGee glanced over at Gwen, who pointedly kept her eyes glued to her menu. Finally McGee shrugged and joined the others on the round leather stools lining the counter. Zan leaned over and declared in a voice loud enough for Gwen to hear, "You know, I think the problem with the decoy idea was that Gwen is just too good an actress."

"You're right, Zan," McGee answered in the same loud voice. "We wanted to fool the Monster of Mulberry Avenue, but Gwen fooled everybody, including an entire pack of Cub Scouts."

The girls glanced sideways to see Gwen's reaction. By the angle of her head, it was clear she was listening to their conversation.

"I guess it was kind of dumb to think that the Monster would show up just because we wanted to see him," Rocky said.

"It wasn't just dumb," Gwen muttered, still keeping her head down. "It was idiotic."

"I'll tell you what was dumb," McGee said. "Thinking he'd let us tie him up so we could pose for a picture. What did we need a photo for, anyway?"

"To prove to the Bunheads and the boys from St. Luke's that we had captured him," Zan reminded her. "Remember?"

"If that's all we needed the photo for," Mary Bubnik said with a giggle, "we could have just dressed someone up to look like the Monster, and posed with them. Who would have known the difference?"

All of the girls, including Gwen, turned slowly to gape at Mary Bubnik.

Rocky shook her head in awe. "Mary Bubnik, you are a genius!"

Mary Bubnik looked back at them in confusion. "What did I say?"

"I think it could really work," McGee said, a note of excitement creeping into her voice. "We know what the Monster looks like, right?"

Zan nodded. "I've kept very detailed notes," she said, tapping her lavender pad.

"We've got the rope, the camera, and shopping bags," McGee continued. "All we'd need to do is get the stuff to dress one of us up like the Monster of Mulberry Avenue."

"Where would we get that?" Mary Bubnik asked.

Zan flipped through the pages of her notepad until she reached one with the words SUSPECT'S DE-

SCRIPTION neatly printed across the top. "We'd need a skeleton mask and a green fright wig."

"Piece of cake," Rocky interrupted. "They sell those at Woolworth's."

Zan made a note on her pad, then continued to read. "A big, black cape."

"We could borrow Dracula's from the theatre," McGee suggested. "There's no rehearsal tonight. All the lead dancers rehearsed this afternoon. He'd never miss it."

"But how do we get in the building?" Mary Bubnik asked.

"Thaddeus Taylor's supposed to be there all the time, guarding things," Rocky said. "We'll just tell him that I forgot my coat yesterday, and I need to get it."

"But aren't we forgetting something important?" Mary Bubnik said. "The Monster is supposed to be seven feet tall. Zan's the tallest of us all, and she's only five feet three."

"Mary's right," Rocky said glumly. "We'll look like the Midget of Mulberry Avenue, instead of the Monster."

No one knew what to say. They sat in silence, completely stumped.

Then the kitchen door swung open and Hi swept in, carrying a platter with a huge ball of orange ice cream shaped like a pumpkin sitting in the center of it. The pumpkin's eyes were gum drops, with a thick marshmallow stuck in the center to make a nose. The mouth was made of rows of little orange-and-white candy corns, laid out in a happy grin.

"I was saving this as a surprise for Halloween," Hi told them as he passed out spoons, "but I think you girls could use this now."

The gang stared at the pumpkin sundae that grinned back at them, and tried to look pleased.

"It looks beautiful, Hi," Mary Bubnik finally said.

Hi looked at them in surprise. "Thank you. But I must confess I expected a little more enthusiasm than this."

"Gee, we're sorry, Hi," Rocky said. "The pumpkin is really cool. But we're kind of depressed."

"I know," Hi said. "That's why I made the sundae."

"The trouble is, we've got a real problem," McGee explained. "And ice cream won't help."

"Well, maybe I can," Hi said, leaning forward on the counter. "What's the matter?"

Zan took a deep breath, then said, "We need to make a short person become a tall person by tonight."

Hi raised his eyebrows. "You're kidding, aren't you?"

All four shook their heads solemnly.

"If we don't," Rocky declared, "McGee's party will be a disaster."

"We'll lose our bet with Courtney," McGee added.

"And we'll have to leave the Academy forever," Mary Bubnik concluded.

"Boy, that *is* a problem," Hi said, scratching his head thoughtfully. "Sounds like you need some outside advice." He gestured with his head toward Gwen in the back booth. "Remember, two heads are better than one."

"That's it!" Gwen slammed her fist on the table with a bang. Her cry startled Zan so much that she nearly fell off her stool. Gwen slid out of her booth and hurried up to the counter. The gang shrank back, waiting for Gwen to let them have it. Instead, she said, "If one of us draped the cape around herself, then sat on someone else's shoulders, we'd look at least seven feet tall."

"What a great idea!" McGee cried, slapping Gwen on the back enthusiastically.

"Of course," Zan exclaimed. "Then one of us could take the picture — "

"I'll do that," Gwen cut in. She grabbed a spoon and scooped up a huge bite of ice cream. Before popping it into her mouth, she grinned at her friends. "I've had enough of being the center of attention."

The girls all giggled and, picking up the remaining spoons, attacked the pumpkin sundae with a vengeance.

"I'll hold Mary Bubnik on my shoulders," McGee

said as she wiped a drip of ice cream off her chin with her hand. "She's the lightest."

"And we can tie you up and pose for the picture," Zan and Rocky chimed in.

"This is wonderful," Gwen mumbled through a mouthful of ice cream.

Hi smiled modestly and bowed his head. "Why, thank you. It's my own special favorite."

"Not the ice cream," Gwen blurted out. "The plan."

When Hi gave her a wounded look, Gwen added quickly, "Your sundae is great, too. But everything you make is always delicious."

"Oh, look!" Mary Bubnik squealed. "The inside is filled with blackberry jam."

The old man's eyes shone happily. "That's my secret ingredient. Keep going," he urged them. "It gets better and better."

For the next few minutes, the gang carved away at the ice cream pumpkin until the only sound in the restaurant was the scrape of their spoons against the empty metal platter.

"I think I just gained ten pounds," Gwen declared, finally pushing the bowl away. She patted her tummy in contentment. "But it was worth it."

The others nodded in agreement. Suddenly, McGee looked up at the clock and shouted, "Geez

Louise, I didn't realize it was so late. We've got to get to the theatre before Thad leaves."

"We'd better hurry," Mary Bubnik added. "My mom will be worried if I don't come home by seven."

"Come on," Rocky shouted, leaping off the stool. Then she clutched her stomach and groaned, "Ooooh, I think I ate too much!"

"Me, too," McGee agreed. "I feel like a slug."

"Let's sit here for just a minute," Gwen insisted, not budging from her stool. "Isn't that the rule? You're not supposed to do anything physical for at least a half an hour after you eat."

"That's for swimming, not walking," Zan observed. She snapped her tapestry bag shut and said, "Let's go."

Reluctantly, Gwen slid off her stool and followed the others to the coatrack by the front door.

Gwen lifted her grandmother's black-and-white coat off the rack and froze in her tracks. Leaning against several boxes of supplies was a large, white cloth bag. Chinese characters had been printed on it in bright red ink. Her eyes widened as she saw that it had stout rope handles sewn into either side. "This is perfect!" she crowed.

"What are you talking about?" McGee asked.

"This," Gwen explained, tugging at the heavy sack with little success. "It's the perfect trick-or-treat bag."

"But that's my rice supply for the week," Hi said.

"Oh, that's why it's so heavy," Gwen grumbled. "How much rice is in there, anyway?"

"Fifty pounds."

"Fifty pounds?" Gwen's eyes lit up greedily. "Do you realize how long fifty pounds of Halloween candy would last?"

"Gwen, forget it," Rocky said. "It's full of rice."

"Please hurry," Zan said, holding open the door. "We have to get to the theatre."

"All right, all right," Gwen mumbled, pulling on her coat. The girls thanked Hi and then hurried down the street, followed by Gwen, who kept muttering, "If I eat every meal at Hi Lo's for the next four days, and order only rice dishes — rice pudding, rice cakes, fried rice, Rice-A-Roni — I think I could definitely eat fifty pounds."

"Yeah, but then you wouldn't be able to walk," McGee said as they reached the civic auditorium. "We'd need a wheelbarrow to haul you around."

"A wheelbarrow!" Gwen cried with glee. "That's it!"

Chapter Nine

"That's odd," Rocky said, pulling on the handle of the big metal door of the auditorium. The door opened easily. "It should be locked."

"Something must be wrong," Mary Bubnik said nervously. "Maybe we'd better not go inside."

"Don't be such a scaredy-cat," Gwen said. "Thad probably forgot to lock it. Let's face it, he's not the greatest guard in the world."

"Someone better tell him about the door," Rocky said, stepping into the building. She was carrying a big paper bag from Woolworth's that held a skeleton mask and green fright wig. They had stopped at the store on their way to the theatre. "Come on."

The girls stood just inside the door, listening in the darkness. The security guard's office was only a few feet down the hall to the left. Light spilled into the corridor and the roar of a crowd at a sports event could be heard from the TV.

"Hey, I bet Thad's watching the Ohio State-Michigan game," McGee said, moving boldly toward the open door. "Let's go see."

"Be careful, McGee," Mary Bubnik whispered from the back of the line.

McGee peeked around the edge of the door and started to chuckle. She gestured for the others to join her. "Come look at this, you guys."

They found the security guard fast asleep in his big swivel chair. His feet were propped up on his desk and a newspaper lay on the floor beside him. He snored steadily as his chest rose and fell with his breathing.

Gwen joined McGee in the doorway and shook her head in disgust. "Anybody could waltz in here, rob this theatre blind, and ol' Lightnin' wouldn't know the difference."

Suddenly, Zan grabbed McGee's arm and said, "Look what's sitting on his desk!"

McGee examined the clutter strewn across the top of the gray metal desk. "A Styrofoam coffee cup, an ashtray, a take-out bag from a burger stand, what looks like a week's worth of newspapers, and a..."

She paused and looked at Zan. "A billfold."

Zan nodded slowly. "A *woman's* billfold."

Mary Bubnik's eyes practically popped out of their sockets. "You don't think he's — ?"

She never finished her sentence because Rocky had clapped her hand over her mouth. But it was too late. Thad snorted in his sleep and his eyes opened wide. He saw the girls staring at him and bolted out of his chair, losing his hat and knocking over the trash can.

"What the heck do you kids think you're doing here?" he demanded in a deep, booming voice.

"Uh, I forgot my coat in the costume shop," Rocky said quickly, "and I have to get it 'cause my school's going on a field trip tomorrow."

Thad squinted one eye at her, trying to decide if she was telling the truth. He ran his hand through the spare threads of dark hair covering his bald head. "You should know better than to break into a building and scare a guy half to death. What if I had pulled my gun?"

"We're sure glad you didn't," McGee said brightly. "It's just that the theatre door was unlocked and we thought you might want to know about it."

"Oh, that." Thad dismissed the subject with a wave of his hand. "I left that open for my wife. She brought me my dinner a little while ago."

"Then we can assume *that* is her billfold over

there?" Zan's voice was as crisp and businesslike as she imagined Tiffany Truenote's would have sounded if she had been on the case.

Thad spun around sharply and stared at his cluttered desk. Then he squinted suspicously at Zan. "Yes, young lady, you can assume that. She left it here by accident." He changed the subject by checking his watch. "I don't have time to mess with you kids. I'm a busy man."

Gwen arched her eyebrows at the television set and said dryly, "We can see that."

Thaddeus Taylor walked over to a big metal panel just outside his office, flipped open the little metal door, and pressed several switches. A loud hum filled the air and the stage and backstage areas were flooded with light. "I've turned on the lights for you," he said brusquely. "Now, get in there and find your coat."

"Thank you, Mr. Taylor," Zan said. "It may take a little while because Rocky isn't quite sure where she left it." She nudged Rocky with her elbow. "Isn't that right, Rocky?"

"Oh, yeah," Rocky said, realizing what Zan was up to. They needed to buy some time to put on the cape and pose for the picture. "It could be in the costume shop, or in one of the dressing rooms. But I know it's around here somewhere, and Dad said not to come home till I found it."

Thad rubbed his chin and his stubble made a scratchy sound. "Well, do the best you can. But stop by here before you leave, so I'll know you're out of the building."

"Yes, sir!" Rocky replied.

The girls hurried directly across the broad stage, passing through the set that was used in the beginning of the ballet. It was the town square of a Transylvanian village and consisted of brightly painted house fronts clustered around a stone fountain. The backdrop hanging behind the set was painted with a picture of a craggy mountain, with Dracula's gloomy castle perched at the peak.

"This is what it looks like when the Bunheads do their dance," Mary Bubnik said. "It's much prettier than our set."

"It may be prettier," Rocky answered, "but ours is a lot more scary, and that's what this ballet's all about."

"A big, gray tomb," Gwen said sourly. "I think it's boring."

"Not with all those flashing lights and weird music," McGee said. "I overheard Courtney say it looked really frightening, and that it was one of her favorite parts of the ballet."

"She only said that because the boys from St. Luke's are out there with us," Gwen retorted.

McGee shrugged her shoulders. "All I know is,

whenever we do our dance, all the other dancers gather backstage to watch."

"That's just because they want to see Armand make his first entrance," Gwen persisted.

"I think it looks so cool," Rocky added, "when that coffin lid opens and he flies straight up in the air."

"Ahem." Zan cleared her throat from the edge of the stage. "Aren't we forgetting what we're here for? We don't have much time."

The girls immediately stopped talking and hurried to catch up with Zan. They clattered down the steps to the costume shop and Rocky flicked on the light switch. "Okay, grab the cape and let's get this over with."

Gwen pushed her glasses up on her nose and peered around the room. "I don't see it."

"Well, it's got to be here somewhere," McGee said. "I'll check Armand's dressing room." She hurried out of the shop and padded down the hall. In the meantime, the girls searched the dozens of costume racks lining the aisles between the sewing machines, and peeked inside the changing rooms at each end of the room.

"Look at these," Mary said, slipping her feet into a pair of soft, black leather boots. "They're Armand Van Valkenberg's. He sure has big feet!" She stumbled across the floor, imitating the dancer in his solo. "Look at me. I'm Count Dracula!"

The laughter of the others encouraged Mary Bubnik to attempt one of Armand's tremendous turns with his leg extended to the side. She tripped and landed on her bottom on the linoleum floor and one of the boots flew off, landing right at Zan's feet.

Zan sat cross-legged on the floor and examined it. "Hmmm," she murmured, pursing her lips. "That's very interesting."

"What?" Gwen asked, kneeling beside her.

"Armand's foot is exactly the same size as the footprint we saw in the alley behind Polar Bear Ice Cream." Zan held the boot up in the air. "See? Size twelve."

"Good," Rocky declared, taking the boot and then yanking the other one off Mary Bubnik's foot. "We'll use his boots for the photo. That'll make it look more convincing."

McGee reentered the costume shop with her arms held out in front of her, cradling a thick pile of black shiny material.

"I found the cape," she said. "It looks like the costume people were cleaning it in his dressing room." She set the huge cape on top of the cutting table. "Look, there's mud on the lining." She flipped over the cape, revealing the bright red satin inside.

Zan leaped to her feet. "I don't remember there being any mud on the set. How could that have gotten there?"

"That's easy," Rocky replied. "It's stage mud."

"Stage mud?" Mary Bubnik repeated. "What's that?"

"It's really brown paint," Rocky explained. "They splatter it on an actor's costume and from the audience, it looks like real mud."

"This doesn't look fake to me," Zan said, rubbing her fingers over the stain. It turned into a fine brown powder in her hand. "I'd say it was pretty fresh — about a day old."

"Maybe Armand stepped outside for some fresh air yesterday," Gwen suggested. "He does spend a lot of time cooped up in that coffin."

"I don't know," Mary Bubnik said, shaking her head. "It sounds suspicious to me."

"Everything sounds suspicious to you." Gwen picked up the Polaroid camera. "Come on, we'd better take the picture before Thad comes looking for us."

McGee grabbed the cape and Rocky grabbed the paper bag while Mary Bubnik scooped up the black leather boots. The girls followed Zan and Gwen toward the back of the theatre where a green exit light glowed in the dark. Zan pushed open the heavy metal door and whispered, "We'll take the picture in the alley where no one will see us."

The girls stepped out onto the loading dock, which was used to bring the sets into the theatre, and found

76

themselves in a harsh circle of light emitted by the security lamp.

Digging into the Woolworth's bag, McGee handed Mary Bubnik the skeleton mask and green wig. "Put these on. Then get on my shoulders."

McGee hurried down the concrete steps to the alley level, slipped her feet into Armand's boots, and braced herself against the concrete. Mary Bubnik slipped the mask over her face, then jammed the wig securely on her head. Two blue eyes peered out from the skeleton face. "I hope nobody sees me like this."

"Don't worry," Zan reassured her. "Even if they did, they wouldn't recognize you."

"Okay, Mary, put your legs over my shoulders," McGee said.

Mary could barely see through the small eyeholes in the mask, but she was able to straddle McGee's neck with her legs. Then she wrapped her hands around McGee's head for support.

"Cut it out," McGee barked. "You're blinding me."

"Sorry," Mary Bubnik said, "but I don't want to fall."

Rocky draped the cape around Mary's shoulders and snapped it under her chin. Gwen picked up the Polaroid and said, "Okay, McGee, move away from the steps and lean against the brick wall. We don't want anybody to recognize the theatre."

McGee, struggling with the weight of Mary Bubnik on her shoulders, staggered over to the wall, mumbling, "Maybe this wasn't such a great idea after all. You weigh a ton."

Zan clapped her hands together in delight. "You two look very convincing."

"Cut the compliments, and take the picture," McGee snapped. "My back is killing me."

Rocky looped her rope around the cape. "This'll show that we captured the Monster of Mulberry Avenue." Then she struck her best karate pose in front of the tall figure.

Zan stood on the opposite side and tried to imagine how Tiffany Truenote would look when she captured a criminal. Zan flipped up the collar of her trench coat and turned sideways, so her profile would be in the picture.

"Hold it!" Gwen shouted, as a breeze whisked down the alley. It picked up several pieces of paper and lifted the edge of the cape just as the flash went off.

The little negative slid out of the camera and Zan and Rocky rushed over to watch it develop.

"How does it look?" Mary Bubnik called from behind the mask. "I didn't know whether to smile or not."

"Geez Louise," McGee muttered. "It doesn't matter. You're wearing a mask."

"Oh, no!" Zan exclaimed as the picture came into view. "The cape blew open. You can see McGee's face as clear as day. And that's definitely Mary's pink-and-blue-striped jacket."

"Don't worry, I'll tear it up," Gwen said, and set the picture on the cement platform. "We'll just take another one."

Zan and Rocky once again assumed their poses. Gwen licked a finger and held it in the air. "No wind," she declared. "I'm going to take it." The flash went off and she said, "We'd better do one more, just to be on the safe side."

Just then the security guard stuck his head out the back door and yelled, "What's going on out here?"

McGee tried to turn to face the wall just as Mary attempted to hop off her shoulders. The two of them fell to the ground in a tangle of legs and black satin.

"Nothing's going on out here," Gwen said, as she tucked the camera and picture behind her back.

"We were just trying on the Dracula cape," Rocky explained. "Because it's so cool."

"Don't you kids know you're supposed to leave other people's things alone?" Thaddeus shook his head impatiently. "Now put that cape back, and get on home where you belong."

After the security guard had disappeared inside

79

the building, Rocky mumbled, "Boy, is he a grump today."

McGee managed to free herself from the cape and hurried to Gwen's side. "Let me see the pictures."

Gwen held up the second one she had taken, and then turned to get the bad one. But it was gone. "Did anybody take that first shot?"

Zan shook her head. "The last I saw, it was lying on the top step."

"Oh, no," Gwen moaned. "It must have blown away."

"What?" the others chorused.

"Well, that's just great," Rocky said, throwing up her hands in disgust. "Now it's too dark to find it."

"We've got to find it," Zan insisted. "What if someone gets a hold of it? They'll know we faked the picture."

"Don't worry," McGee reassured her. "They won't. Who hangs out in this alley, anyway? Besides, the garbage guys come on Tuesdays. They'll pick it up and throw it away." She gathered the cape up in her arms. "We'd better get out of here before Thaddeus Taylor comes back and really gets mad."

Mary Bubnik had been studying the picture intently. "Boy, this is really convincing," she said with a giggle. "It actually looks like you two captured the Monster of Mulberry Avenue."

Rocky peered at the photograph over her shoulder. "It does, doesn't it?" She smiled with satisfaction. "Now all we have to do is show this to Tyson, and then tell him we took it after we captured the Monster."

"And then we tell him the harrowing story of how the Monster suddenly broke out of his ropes and ran away," Zan concluded.

"Do you think Tyson and his friends will believe us?" Mary Bubnik asked.

"If he doesn't," McGee said, sticking the special photo in her pocket, "our dancing days are finished."

Chapter Ten

Tyson Bickle stared intently at the photo Gwen had handed him. It was Friday night and he and his friends had agreed to come early to the theatre to meet with the gang. From the looks on their faces, the boys were definitely impressed.

"Is the Monster really seven feet tall?" Clint asked.

The gang exchanged nervous glances.

"He may even be taller," Rocky said. "Closer to eight feet. Right?"

The others nodded their heads solemnly.

"He's a giant," Mary Bubnik added for good measure. "No doubt about it."

"Now tell us once more how you captured him,"

Tyson asked, turning the photograph over in his hands.

The girls turned to Zan to tell the story they'd carefully worked out together. "Last night," Zan began, "at exactly eighteen hundred hours — "

"That's military talk for six p.m.," Rocky explained.

" — we were at Baumgartner's," Zan continued, "picking up some makeup for the play."

"Remember?" McGee cut in. "Miss Hamilton, the head costumer, said we needed to get some eyebrow pencils and stuff like that."

Zan took a deep breath. "We had just come out of the department store and were cutting through the alley to get to Main Street when . . ." She paused dramatically. "It happened!"

"What happened?" all three boys cried.

"The Monster of Mulberry Avenue leaped out from behind a Dumpster," Zan said, her brown eyes dancing with excitement.

"And howled at us like a demon," Gwen added.

"He flailed his arms around in the air, like they were tentacles on an octopus," Zan said.

"Yeah," Rocky cut in. "It's like he didn't have any bones or joints."

"And then he yelled 'boo!' " McGee whispered.

"We just didn't know what to do," Mary Bubnik added breathlessly. "Why, personally, I was just paralyzed with fear."

"But McGee saw the rope," Rocky said, "and quick as a wink, she wrapped it around him tight as a drum."

"He must not have noticed that there were five of us," Zan added, "because McGee ducked behind the Dumpster and then crawled on her hands and knees to get behind the Monster."

"Wow!" Tyson said, shaking his head in admiration. "You did that?"

McGee blushed and stared at her feet. When they had invented the story, they had agreed that it was best if McGee was the one to have captured the Monster. That way, the boys from St. Luke's would be sure to come to her party.

Courtney Clay, who'd been sulking with her friends in the far corner of the costume shop, called out abruptly, "How was it that you just *happened* to have a camera?"

Zan was ready for that question. "That's the truly amazing part," she replied. "You see, Gwen's mother was having her Polaroid camera repaired at Blatchley's camera store and she had asked Gwen to pick it up for her."

"Hmmph." Courtney leaned back against one of the makeup tables with her arms folded across her chest.

"If you really captured the Monster, how come we

didn't read about it in the newspapers?" Page Tuttle asked.

"He got away," McGee said simply.

"The Monster escaped?" Clint asked.

Zan nodded. "You see, McGee and Mary Bubnik ran to call the police while Gwen took the picture. While they were gone, the Monster broke the rope that was holding him."

"Like the Incredible Hulk," Gwen added.

"What did you do then?" Joel asked.

"Well, we got awfully scared," Zan said. "And Gwen fainted."

"I what?" Gwen looked at Zan in shock. This was news to her. According to the story they'd agreed upon, Gwen had tried to capture the Monster single-handedly, but was thrown against a wall and knocked unconscious.

"You fainted," Zan repeated, looking meaningfully at Gwen. "Remember?"

"Oh, uh . . . yeah," Gwen sputtered. Then she added, "From hunger. Otherwise, I would have chased after the Monster and tried to recapture him."

"A likely story," Courtney sniffed. "I don't believe a word of it."

"It sounds pretty incredible," Tyson agreed. "But here's the evidence." He held up the photograph. "See for yourself, Courtney."

Courtney minced across the room and leaned in as close as she could to Tyson to look at the picture. Rocky snorted in disgust. Courtney hardly looked at it but stared up at the handsome boy and said in a sickeningly sweet voice, "Gee, Ty, I guess you're right."

Tyson hardly noticed she was there. He smiled right at McGee and, gesturing to the photograph, said, "This took a lot of courage. Really excellent."

"No kidding," Clint agreed. He and Joel stared at the gang in awe.

Suddenly, the door to the room burst open and a disheveled figure dressed in a purple coat and a red turban staggered into the room.

"Water," she gasped, sinking into the nearest empty chair. "Somebody, please get me a glass of water. I've just been booed!"

"Miss Delacorte, are you okay?" Zan cried, grasping the old woman's hand.

Miss Delacorte was the Academy's receptionist and long ago had been a ballerina with the Ballet Russe. She was the gang's eccentric friend who often invited them to her apartment for Russian tea and marzipan cookies.

"My heart feels like it is try-ink to leap out of my chest," the lady rasped in her thick Russian accent. "And my knees feel like pud-dink."

"I think you mean Jell-O," Zan corrected.

"That's the word," Miss Delacorte said, pointing one long, bony hand at Zan. Her fingers were covered in rings set with large amethysts and little tiny diamonds.

McGee raced to the sink, filled a paper cup with water, and brought it to the old woman.

Tyson sprang forward. "Where did the attack happen?"

"Out there somewhere." Miss Delacorte fluttered her hand in the general direction of the alley.

Tyson turned to Clint and Joel with a grin. "Come on, guys, what are we waiting for? This is our chance to grab the Monster." The three boys disappeared out the door without a backward glance.

"Here, Miss Delacorte, drink this." McGee handed the lady the cup of water. "And try to calm down."

Rocky grabbed a magazine off the nearest table and fanned the lady with it. "Don't just stand there," she barked at Courtney and Page, "call the security guard."

The Bunheads hurried out of the dressing room. The moment they were gone, Gwen turned to Zan and hissed, "Why did you change our story and say I fainted?"

"I could tell by the looks on their faces that they'd never believe you raced after the Monster," Zan explained. "It was starting to sound a little too much like a comic book."

"Well, thanks a lot," Gwen retorted. "Now the boys from St. Luke's think I'm just a big wimp."

Rocky, who was still fanning Miss Delacorte, leaned forward and said, "Take a couple of deep breaths. You'll feel a lot better."

Gwen opened her blue dance bag with the embroidered, pink toe shoes on it and pulled out half a bologna sandwich. "Eat something first," she advised. "I always find a little bite after a bad scare really settles me down."

"Thank you, dear," Miss Delacorte said, taking a nibble out of the sandwich. "I hope you're right."

Zan reached for her lavender pad and pen and knelt beside the older woman. "Miss Delacorte, can you remember what your assailant looked like?"

"But of course I can," Miss Delacorte sniffed, dabbing some crumbs from her lips with her hankie. "He took my purse, not my mind."

"He stole your purse?" Mary Bubnik gasped in dismay. "Was there a lot of money in it?"

"But of course not." Miss Delacorte took the magazine from Rocky and began fanning herself. "I never carry money in my purse. You should know that, Mary Bubnik."

"What do you carry?" McGee asked out of curiosity.

"Birdseed," Miss Delacorte replied. "For Miss Myna."

They all knew Miss Myna was the receptionist's pet myna bird, who spent a good deal of time at the ballet studio.

"She likes to unhook the snap and reach inside, you know," Miss Delacorte explained.

There was a flurry of activity as the seamstresses hurried into the costume shop, carrying the clothes that needed last-minute repairs. Zan ignored the distraction and persisted with her questions. "Was there anything about the Monster that you found unusual?"

Miss Delacorte paused. "Everything. He had a skeleton face, green hair, and those strange glowink feet."

"Glowing feet?" Zan repeated. There had never been a mention of that in any of the other reports. "Are you sure?"

"Of course I am sure." Miss Delacorte took another nibble of the sandwich Gwen had offered her. "How could I ever forget such a horrible sight?"

As she spoke, the old lady's hunger seemed to increase and Gwen watched in dismay as she devoured the rest of the sandwich and then reached for Gwen's emergency bag of corn chips. Miss Delacorte tore open the bag and, after popping a handful in her mouth, added, "He had these black shoes with little spots of yellow and green that glowed in the dark."

"Anything else?" Zan asked, scribbling furiously to take it all down.

Miss Delacorte nodded. "He was also wearing a big black cape — just like that one over there." She pointed to Dracula's black satin cape that Miss Hamilton had just draped over a standing dummy.

"Look at the hem!" Mary Bubnik's eyes were two big circles in her face. "It's covered in mud."

"I just don't understand where this dirt is coming from," Miss Hamilton said, rubbing some cleaning solution on the stain with a rag. "And Armand says he knows nothing about it."

"That's what he *says*," Mary whispered ominously.

The sound of heavy footsteps treading down the hall caught their attention, along with a jangling of what sounded like keys. Then Courtney Clay appeared in the door, smiling smugly.

"I thought you were going to get Thad," Rocky said.

"He wasn't around," Courtney replied. "But I found something much better." She held out her hand and whispered, "Ta-da!"

The heavy footsteps stopped and two police officers, with guns and handcuffs at their hips, stepped through the door. A man in a tan trench coat and a slouch hat followed them inside. The girls could see two more policemen still outside in the hall.

"Wow, it's not just the police, but the entire force," Gwen gasped.

"Detective Pinskey," the man in the trench coat growled, flashing a wallet with a silver badge. He chewed on a thick cigar that sent clouds of acrid smoke all over the room. "Check it out," he said to the officers, gesturing with his cigar to the room.

"Wha — what are *you* guys doing here?" Rocky stammered. "We didn't call you."

"My men followed a trail of footsteps and discarded shopping bags in the alley outside that led us to this theatre."

As the detective spoke, the uniformed officers peeked behind curtains, opened closets, and poked their noses into every corner of the costume shop.

"I don't want to scare you," he added, "but we have reason to believe that the mugger people call the Monster of Mulberry Avenue is hiding somewhere in this building."

Chapter Eleven

"This is an outrage! Tonight is our opening!" Mr. Anton declared. The ballet director stood fuming on the stage, as the police poked around the set. He cut an impressive figure in his black tuxedo that he wore specifically for first nights. The rest of the ballet company stood in a group behind him. They'd put on leg warmers over their tights, and draped sweat-shirts and towels around their upper bodies.

"Do you hear me, Detective Pinskey?" Mr. Anton flipped his glasses to the top of his thick shock of silver hair and glared at the policeman, who was lounging comfortably in a front-row seat while his men worked. "A complete outrage. We have an audience in less than an hour."

"I'm sorry, Mr. Anton. What more can I say?" the detective replied with a shrug. "We're just doing our jobs."

"How am I supposed to prepare this company for opening night with these continual disruptions?" the director ranted, his penetrating eyes shooting daggers at the detective. "On Tuesday we were delayed because of a power failure, and now the police are tearing our theatre apart."

"We're doing our best to leave things just as we found them," the detective replied, taking a long puff of his cigar.

"Oh?" Mr. Anton raised his eyebrows as he pointed to the scattered set pieces behind the dancers. "The entire town square has been moved three feet to the right. You call this leaving things as you found them?"

"I'm sorry," the detective said. "But my men need to look everywhere." A thick cloud of his cigar smoke drifted up onto the stage, and several dancers began to cough. "We thought our man might be hiding behind those little houses."

"Ridiculous," the director snapped. "And put out that disgusting cigar. Smoking is absolutely prohibited in the auditorium."

"Sure." The detective snuffed out the burning ash of his cigar with his shoe, then stuck the butt back in his mouth.

"I want you to know that we have spent weeks setting lights, choreographing dances, and hanging backdrops," Mr. Anton continued, "only to have your ruffians destroy it in a half hour."

"Hey, Sarge," one of the officers called from the wings, "we've searched this place from top to bottom and can't find a sign of the guy."

The detective scratched his head. "I guess he probably was just passing through." He turned back to Mr. Anton. "Sorry for the inconvenience."

Mr. Anton nodded stiffly.

Detective Pinskey turned back to his men. "Let's see if we can pick up the trail on the other side of the building."

With a loud thundering of shoes, the officers marched across the wooden stage and disappeared out of the auditorium.

"Well!" Mr. Anton took a deep breath. "I'm glad that's over. Now we can get back to work." He clapped his hands loudly. "Dancers, the show will begin in less than half an hour. Prepare yourselves, please."

The professional dancers spread out and lined up along the edges of the stage. Dropping their wraps on the floor, they began doing deep *pliés* and *relevés* to stretch out their muscles, which had gotten tight from standing around. Mr. Anton and several stage-hands moved the tiny painted houses back into their proper positions around the artificial fountain.

McGee and the gang stood together in the wings, listening intently to Zan.

"The police are making a big mistake," she whispered. "They think the Monster is hiding somewhere. Well, he's hiding, all right, but in plain sight."

"What do you mean?" McGee asked.

Zan looked over her shoulders to make sure no one else was listening. "I mean, the Monster of Mulberry Avenue is one of us."

"How can you be so sure?" Rocky demanded.

"Think about it." Zan ticked off each point on her fingers. "Size twelve feet, a cape that looks just like the one in the costume shop, and..." She raised one finger. "I heard Detective Pinskey say that he commits his crimes between five and seven o'clock at night."

Gwen's eyes widened behind her glasses. "That's just before we come to the theatre."

"Right. But the Monster never does anything between seven and nine p.m."

"Why do you think he doesn't?" Mary Bubnik asked.

"Because he's too busy rehearsing," Zan explained.

"You mean, you think he's one of the dancers?"

Zan shook her head. "Not just one of them, but *the* dancer."

"You mean *Dracula*?" all four of them gasped.

Zan nodded. "It's got to be."

Mary Bubnik narrowed her eyes. "I knew I didn't trust that guy."

"But couldn't it be any other dancer?" McGee wondered.

"Well, I was thinking that," Zan admitted. "But then I kept an eye on Armand Van Valkenberg while the police were searching the theatre."

"Gee, I didn't even see him on the stage," Mary Bubnik said.

"He wasn't," Zan said. "He was standing over by the lighting control panel." She pointed to the metal board where the stage manager and lighting man sat during the performance. It sat just behind the curtains of the stage. "He could see the detective and the police, but they couldn't see him."

"This is too creepy to be believed," McGee said with a shudder. "And just imagine, we've been dancing with that guy for weeks."

"That's right!" Mary Bubnik's eyes grew huge with a sudden realization. "Why, he could have just reached out and bitten our necks at any time and sucked our veins dry."

Rocky rolled her eyes at the ceiling. "He's a purse thief, Mary, not a vampire."

"How do you know that?" Mary Bubnik retorted. "Scaring old women and taking their handbags could be just the beginning."

"What should we do?" Gwen whispered. "Turn him in?"

Zan shook her head. "We don't really have anything solid against him right now. The police would just laugh at us. We need to get some hard evidence."

"Evidence!" a nasal voice called from behind them. "I'll show you evidence."

The group spun around to find Courtney sneering at them, flanked by Alice and Page. Courtney thrust a small photograph in front of the gang's faces. "There it is, in living color."

The girls stared at the tiny Polaroid picture of Rocky and Zan posed in front of the Monster. It looked almost like the one they'd shown the boys from St. Luke's. But unfortunately it was a little bit different. In this picture, McGee was clearly visible, squinting at the camera as the wind blew open the black cape.

"Where'd you get that?" Rocky demanded.

"Mr. Taylor had it on his desk," Courtney replied. "I'm sure he was about to telephone the police to tell them about this."

97

"So why didn't he?"

"I told him to wait," Courtney said. "The ballet comes first. I didn't want him to ruin Mr. Anton's opening night."

"Gee, that was thoughtful of you," Gwen said sarcastically.

"Besides, I needed to telephone my mother," Courtney added with a superior smile. "She's bringing in some photographers from the paper." Her eyes glinted triumphantly. "It's not every day that a sixth-grader captures a town menace. Mother thought it would be good publicity for the Academy, and also look good on my college applications."

"Oh, brother," McGee said, clapping her hand to her forehead. "You've got to be kidding."

"Does she look like she's kidding?" Page pointed at Courtney, whose mouth was set in a hard line.

"Come on, get real," Rocky said, stepping forward. "You don't actually think we would go around frightening little old ladies just to get their purses, do you?"

The Bunheads nodded in unison.

"Yes, I do," Courtney said. "Everyone knows you're practically a juvenile delinquent, Rocky Garcia. And so will the police when they see this picture."

Rocky lunged for the photo. "Give me that!"

Courtney leaped back out of the way and called out, "Mr. Taylor! Help!" Then she turned and hissed, "I knew you'd try something like this."

The lanky security guard stepped out of the shadows from backstage. He reached for the photo and tucked it into the front pocket of his uniform. "I'll take care of this," he said, patting his pocket. Then he narrowed his eyes at the girls. "The police know how to deal with rotten kids like you."

"What!" Rocky howled.

"But we haven't done anything," Mary Bubnik protested.

"Courtney, this is truly getting out of hand," Zan said urgently. "There is a logical explanation for that photo."

"I don't have time to listen to your phony stories," Courtney sniffed. "The ballet is about to begin and *I* have a performance to give."

"I thought you just gave one," Gwen cracked, "doing your dumb impression of a detective."

"Ha-ha." A broad smile spread across Courtney's face. "We'll see who's laughing once the police put you away."

"You'll be laughing out the other side of your face," Rocky snarled, "after I knock that silly grin around to the back of your head."

She clenched her fist but McGee grabbed her by the arm and held her back. "You're completely off base," McGee shouted at Courtney. "We have proof that we're not the Monster."

"What proof?" Page demanded.

99

"We were all with you when Miss Delacorte got booed earlier today," McGee replied. "Remember?"

Courtney hesitated for a second, then hurriedly conferred with Page and Alice. Finally she raised her head. "Miss Delacorte is your friend. I'll bet you had her fake that attack to give you an alibi."

"That's the dumbest thing I've ever heard," Gwen muttered.

"Just try using her to defend you," Courtney shot back. "That old thing can barely remember her own name, let alone where she was this afternoon."

The girls exchanged worried looks. Courtney's charge was cruel . . . but partly true. Miss Delacorte had a reputation for being forgetful, especially about times and places.

Courtney smoothed out her long, blue skirt and smiled sweetly. "Oh, by the way — I showed Tyson Bickle the picture."

"What did he say?" McGee asked, squeezing her eyes shut and waiting to hear the worst.

"I believe he called you a bunch of liars," Courtney said, smoothing a stray hair into her bun. "And I told him he was right. You've always been liars, but now you are also thieves."

"Places, everyone, for the start of the show," the stage manager's voice crackled over the intercom.

"I guess we'd better get in place," Courtney said. "Don't try to escape. Thad is guarding the exits until the police come." Then she turned and flounced toward the wings.

Page and Alice followed, calling back over their shoulders in mocking tones, "Break a leg!"

"I know a leg I'd like to break," Rocky muttered.

"I knew something terrible was going to happen," Mary Bubnik moaned. "And this is it. The police are going to arrest us, and nobody will believe our story." Her large blue eyes welled up with tears. "Oh, this is just awful!"

McGee took hold of the small blonde by the shoulders and shook her gently. "It doesn't help getting hysterical, Mary. We have to think calmly and clearly."

"I'm thinking calmly and clearly," Gwen declared. "And from where I sit, things look *really* bad."

"I hate to say this," Zan said, "but unless we can find positive proof that Armand is the real Monster by the end of the show, we probably will be arrested."

"And go to jail," Rocky said.

Courtney stuck her head out from the wings and whispered, "That's right. You'll be behind bars for the rest of your lives. And, personally, I can't think of a better place for you to be."

101

Chapter Twelve

The girls stood glumly in the wings, waiting for their entrance cue. Normally they would have been jittery with stage fright on an opening night, but their minds were occupied with other, more unsettling, thoughts. Like prison.

McGee was haunted by the thought of never playing hockey or baseball again. Mary Bubnik saw herself in a striped convict's uniform, pounding rocks with a sledgehammer. Gwen could only think of having to eat lumpy, gray prison food that tasted like paste.

Rocky couldn't get her father's disappointed look out of her mind. Her dad was a sergeant in the Air

Force security police. When he found out that his only daughter was a crook, he'd never forgive her.

Zan felt her cheeks burn with shame and humiliation. Tiffany Truenote would *never* have gotten herself, let alone four of her friends, into a mess like this. Zan knew she had to think of a way out of it.

Their cue came and McGee led them onto the dimly lit stage. As fog poured out of the dry-ice machines, Dracula's tomb rose up from a trap door beneath the stage. Lightning flashed above their heads and claps of thunder echoed throughout the theatre. The girls ran in figure eights around the stage, raising up on tiptoe with their arms outstretched, and then hunching over and running with their knees bent. The choreography was simple but it created the impression that they actually were bats swooping in circles around the large, elaborately carved coffin.

The gang performed their moves correctly but with hardly any enthusiasm. They were so lost in their own dreadful thoughts that they completely forgot about Dracula's entrance. When the tomb suddenly split into two halves and the tall, imposing figure rose up out of his coffin, Mary Bubnik actually screamed — a long, terrified howl that carried right over the music.

Armand Van Valkenberg was startled by her cry and turned his head sharply to glare at her. His stern look terrified Mary Bubnik so much that she broke formation and circled away from the front edge of the stage.

The rest of the girls had to follow or else it would be obvious that Mary had made a mistake. McGee swooped in right behind the frightened girl and, raising her cape to shield them from view of the audience, hissed, "What do you think you're doing, Mary?"

"Staying away from Dracula!" Mary Bubnik called back over her shoulder.

"We're supposed to surround him, not run from him." McGee grabbed the back of Mary's cape and yanked her back abruptly.

"Stop it!" she gagged, clutching at her throat. "You're choking me."

During the entire exchange, the conductor down in the orchestra pit was gesturing at them frantically with his baton. Gwen, who'd been the last to follow McGee down to the edge of the stage, noticed the conductor's signals and stopped still. Without her glasses, everything was a blur and she squinted at him, trying to decipher what he wanted. Finally Gwen hissed impatiently, "What?"

"Get back upstage," the conductor shouted. *"Now!"*

His voice overpowered the orchestra and several

people in the front row of the audience jumped in their seats.

Rocky raised her arms and swooped in close to Gwen. "Follow me!" she shouted, leading the gang toward the wings.

The music swelled as the thunder and lightning built to a dazzling climax of light and sound, which was the cue for the boys from St. Luke's to make their entrance. As they darted onto the stage, the line of boys nearly collided with Rocky, who was trying to get off.

"Where are you going?" Tyson whispered under the noise. "There's still more dancing to do."

"Do it yourselves," Rocky called as she dashed into the wings. "You can handle it."

McGee dragged Mary Bubnik, who was still clutching at the tie strings around her neck, after Rocky, with Zan right behind them.

"Oh, no, you don't," Gwen called. "You're not leaving me out on this stage all by myself." She caught up with them just as they disappeared into the wings.

The boys from St. Luke's hesitated for just a moment, then struggled on without the girls. Rocky and the others stopped in the wings and watched the boys flounder through the part of the dance where they were supposed to join hands with the girls and weave over and under each other's arms.

"It looks like they're dancing with invisible bats," McGee giggled, as the boys pretended to clutch hands and weave under arms that weren't there.

"Serves them right for siding with the Bunheads," Rocky declared.

"It's lucky there's all that smoke out there," Gwen remarked. "Otherwise, they'd really look stupid."

"I don't think Mr. Anton is going to like this," Mary Bubnik said slowly. "I mean, we just ruined his ballet."

"We!" McGee blinked at Mary Bubnik in amazement. "You're the one who wouldn't dance near Dracula."

"Well, I would have gone on if you hadn't tried to choke me to death," Mary Bubnik replied.

"Can the fighting, you guys," Rocky said. "It doesn't matter. As soon as the show is over, we'll be arrested and probably never see Mr. Anton again."

"Not if I have anything to say about it," Zan said boldly. "I've got an idea that might get us out of hot water."

"You do?" McGee asked anxiously.

Zan nodded. "We'll search Armand's dressing room for incriminating evidence."

Rocky looked disgusted. "Come on, Zan, he'd never let us do that."

"How can he stop us?" Zan pointed to the stage, where the vampire Dracula was hovering above his casket. "Dracula still has to do his dance with the boys from St. Luke's, plus his big solo. That gives us about four minutes."

Zan started to lead the girls behind the backdrop but Rocky stopped her. "Not that way." Rocky pointed across the stage. "Marv, the stage manager's assistant, just left the lighting board, and I think he's heading this way."

The girls turned and pounded down the stairs to the floor beneath the stage. They tiptoed down the hall to the dressing room with the star on it, and slipped inside.

"Quickly," Zan urged, closing the door behind them and switching on the light. "Search the place completely."

"But what are we looking for?" Gwen asked.

"Anything that might associate Armand with the Monster of Mulberry Avenue," Zan replied as she probed the pockets of the dancer's overcoat. "You know, a billfold, a wig, or a skeleton mask."

"He may have hidden them in a dance bag," Rocky pointed out.

McGee held up a black leather satchel. "Like this?"

"Yes!" Zan hurried over and watched excitedly as McGee turned the bag upside down and emptied the contents onto the floor. Several pairs of socks, a turtleneck, several worn pairs of ballet shoes, and a pair of tights fell onto the floor, along with a book.

107

"Here's something." McGee held up the slender volume, which had a green plastic cover that was dog-eared at the corners.

"Ooh, what is it?" Mary Bubnik cried.

Zan flipped eagerly through the pages. *"English Made Easy."* She looked at the girls in disappointment. "It's just a language book."

Meanwhile, Gwen was at the dressing table, rifling through the drawers. "Makeup towel, washcloth, cold cream, pancake base," Gwen muttered as she examined the contents. "And a notepad." She leafed through its pages and declared, "He's scribbled all sorts of stuff in here but it's in a foreign language."

"Probably Dutch," Zan said. "It might be his journal."

"You mean, like a diary?" Mary Bubnik's eyes widened. "Where he's written detailed accounts of how he booed all the old ladies of Deerfield?"

The girls clustered around Gwen, who was still holding the notebook. Zan opened it to the first page, then hesitated.

"I feel really funny about reading someone's personal diary," Zan said. "I mean, I'd hate it if someone read mine."

"This could be important evidence," Gwen insisted. "We'd better take it."

"I would not do that if I were you."

The five girls whirled around so fast that they

knocked over several makeup tubes that had been lined up neatly on the dressing table.

Armand Van Valkenberg stood just inside the dressing room, dressed in his tuxedo and cape. The door was shut behind him.

"Those are my notes about the ballet. I need them for this performance." His eyes blazed with anger but his voice was even and controlled.

"How did you get in here?" Rocky asked in a shaky voice. "We didn't hear you come in."

"That is because you were so busy trying to steal my personal property." The dancer's expression never changed. In fact, his lips barely moved when he spoke. He just stared at them with his steely blue eyes.

"That's not true," Zan protested. "We were looking for evidence — oops!" She clapped her hand over her mouth. "I didn't mean to say that."

"What *did* you mean?"

Armand took a step forward and Mary Bubnik squealed, "You stay away from me, you blood-sucker!"

A thin smile curled up the edges of the man's lips. "Bloodsucker?" he repeated. "Is that what you think I am?"

"That, and a whole lot more," McGee muttered. "Let's talk about being a purse thief."

The smile vanished. "How dare you accuse me

of such a thing!" In one swift move, his hand shot out of his cape and suddenly the dressing room door flew open. "Guard!" the dancer shouted into the hall. "I want these girls removed from my dressing room at once!"

"What's the trouble, Mr. Van Valkenberg?" Thaddeus Taylor asked from the hall. When he stepped into view, the girls could see the edge of the Polaroid picture peeking out from his breast pocket.

"Remove these creatures from my dressing room," Armand declared in his thick accent. "I must go dance. When I return, I expect to see them . . ." He snapped his fingers impatiently, trying to think of the correct word. "Disappeared!" Then the gaunt dancer turned on his heel and, with a flick of his black cape, strode majestically to the stage.

Thaddeus faced the girls and his features tightened. "You!" He gestured with the long flashlight in his hand like a gun. "Get out of there, and put Mr. Van Valkenberg's things back where you found them."

Zan stood her ground. "We're not leaving without this notebook," she said, waving the journal in the air. "I have a feeling we may need it in court."

"Court?" The guard stared at her like she was crazy. "What in the world are you talking about?"

"Look." Zan held out the notebook for the guard

110

to take but it slipped from her hands and fell to the floor beside Thad's boot. She knelt down to pick it up and sucked in her breath sharply.

"What is it, Zan?" Gwen asked when she saw the stunned look on her friend's face.

Zan didn't answer. She stared intently at Thaddeus Taylor's boots until finally she asked, "Mr. Taylor, what size shoe do you wear?"

"Now, what kind of dumb question is that?" the guard muttered.

"Never mind, you don't have to answer," Zan said, looking up at him. "I already know. Size twelve, isn't it?"

"As a matter of fact, yes." By this time Thad was looking thoroughly baffled. "But what's that got to do with anything?"

"Zan!" Gwen gasped. "You don't think he's —?"

Zan didn't let Gwen finish her sentence. She sprang to her feet and declared sternly, "Thaddeus Taylor, I'm placing you under citizen's arrest!"

"What for?" Mary Bubnik asked.

Zan raised her chin and looked the man squarely in the eye. "For the deliberate and cruel booing of old ladies on Mulberry Avenue."

"Geez Louise, Zan!" McGee muttered out the corner of her mouth. "You don't have any proof."

"You want proof?" Zan pointed dramatically at Thad's feet. "There's the evidence, right there!"

111

"Where?" everyone, including Thad, stared down at his foot.

His black shoes were covered with little specks of greenish glow paint.

"There are the glowing feet Miss Delacorte was talking about," Zan said. "And, if you'll look in the cuff of his left pant leg, you'll find a small supply of birdseed, which must have fallen out of the purse he stole from her!"

Thad's jaw dropped open and he stood paralyzed. Mary Bubnik's eyes widened as she realized that Zan was absolutely right. "It *is* you!"

Suddenly, Thaddeus Taylor reached out and switched off the dressing room light. Mary Bubnik screamed as the room was plunged into darkness. The door slammed shut and the girls ran blindly into each other in the confusion.

"Get out of my way," Gwen huffed, flailing her arms in front of her.

"Stop hitting me!" Rocky barked. "And everyone quit moving. I'm trying to find the door."

Finally, Zan found the doorknob and ran out into the hall. She could see Thaddeus Taylor passing a group of dancers at the far end of the corridor.

"Don't let that man get away," Zan shouted. "He's the Monster of Mulberry Avenue!"

Chapter Thirteen

Thaddeus Taylor fled down the narrow hall lined with dressing rooms, his heavy boots clattering loudly across the tiled floor. The boys from St. Luke's were talking together in one of the doorways and looked up in surprise as the guard rushed by.

"Don't let him get away, Ty," McGee shouted desperately. "That's our Monster of Mulberry Avenue."

Tyson Bickle looked first at the guard, who was climbing up the stairs to the stage, and then back at the girls, who were pounding down the hall.

"Sure he is," Tyson drawled.

"We're not kidding," Rocky said, slowing down to

talk to the boys. "We've got the evidence that'll lock him up."

"Don't bother with those idiots," Gwen shouted over her shoulder. "Our man is getting away."

"I'm right behind you." Rocky took the stairs three at a time up to the backstage area.

It was pitch black in the wings and the gang paused to let their eyes adjust to the darkness. On stage, the orchestra was playing a haunting melody as Dracula danced his first *pas de deux* with the ballerina playing Lucy.

"Which way did he go?" Gwen hissed.

Zan scratched her head. "I'm not sure. But logic tells me he would head for an exit." She pointed to her left, where the security guard's office was. "Which is that way."

A policeman was standing just beneath the green exit sign.

"Duck!" Rocky whispered. "It's the cops."

All five girls dove behind the nearest piece of scenery, a large rolling platform that held the tall, three-tiered fountain from the villager scenes. Around the base of the fountain were thick plastic bushes enclosed by a low brick wall.

"Oh, no," Mary Bubnik moaned. "Courtney called the police and they've come to arrest us."

A burst of applause rang out from the auditorium.

Zan peeked out from behind the fountain wall. She watched Armand Van Valkenberg carry a ballerina into the wings. The girl hung limply in his arms and Zan whispered, "Dracula got his first victim, so it must be time for the dance of the villagers."

Suddenly, their hiding place shuddered and began to roll.

"It's an earthquake," Gwen gasped. She threw her arms around McGee and held on for dear life.

As the wooden platform rumbled along the stage floor, Zan raised her head and peered out between the first and second levels of the fountain. "Oh, this is truly, truly terrible!"

Rocky and Mary Bubnik, who were clutching each other, cried out, "What's happening?"

"We're going onto the stage," Zan replied. "This is part of the set for the villagers' scene."

"What?" McGee yelped.

The platform rolled onto the center of the stage and five furry bat heads with little pointy ears raised up and peered over the edge of the fountain. The girls saw the sea of faces out in the audience and quickly ducked back down behind the garden wall, contorting their bodies to stay hidden from view.

But they weren't quick enough. The entire audience saw them, and a wave of chuckling rippled through the auditorium. The villagers parading in front of the fountain had no idea what the audience was laughing about, and shot each other confused looks as they began their dance.

"Do you think they saw us?" Mary Bubnik asked.

"Of course they saw us," Rocky snapped. "Since when do you remember the villager dance being a laugh riot?"

"Well, why are they still laughing?" Zan whispered.

Rocky craned her neck to look behind her and her eyes widened as she saw what was causing the uproar.

"Gwen!" she hissed. "Your butt is sticking out from behind that rock."

Gwen raised up to see and the audience exploded with giggles once more. She scrambled on her hands and knees closer to the gang, running right over McGee, who was lying face down on the floor.

"Why didn't one of you tell me before?" Gwen asked indignantly. "That's really embarrassing."

"Get off me!" McGee mumbled. "You're breaking my back."

"How much longer is this dance?" Mary Bubnik asked from behind a clump of bushes. "I don't think I can hold this position much longer." She had pulled her knees up to her ears, ducking her head between them into a little ball. "I'm not that limber."

"The Bunheads still have to do their number," Zan

whispered. "They should be entering any moment now."

As if on cue, Courtney skipped onto the stage, followed by Page, Alice, and several girls from their dance class. As the Bunheads waltzed over toward the fountain, Zan warned, "Here they come."

Courtney, who was the first to reach the back of the fountain, nearly tripped over Mary Bubnik in surprise. Of course she didn't expect five bodies to be in the path of her dance. Courtney leaped in the air to avoid Mary Bubnik, then lurched sideways to keep from stomping on McGee and Gwen. The audience roared with laughter and Courtney, her face frozen in a tight smile, said, "I'll get you for this."

The other village children were circling around in front of the fountain and hadn't seen Courtney's near misses. One by one they did their lovely waltz steps up to the fountain and then broke into odd jerks and twitches behind it, trying to avoid the girls on the ground.

Page and Alice crashed into each other and ricocheted off in opposite directions, flailing their arms like windmills to catch their balance. Rocky found this so funny that the next time they came around, she deliberately stuck her foot out and tripped them both again.

"This is fun," Rocky whispered. "Why didn't we think of this before?"

"I wish you wouldn't do that," Mary Bubnik moaned. "We're going to get in big trouble."

"What are you worried about?" Gwen retorted. "We're already going to jail. It doesn't get any bigger than that."

A young male dancer strode onto the stage carrying a tall maypole with long, colored ribbons streaming from its top. Courtney and the rest of the Bunheads stopped dancing and clapped their hands together in exaggerated delight. They pointed to the pole and mimed their comments to each other.

As Courtney mouthed imaginary words, McGee called mockingly, "Oh, goody, it's the maypole dance."

As Page opened her mouth to respond, Gwen said, "Why don't we join in? Maybe we'll hang ourselves."

Page shot a dirty look over her shoulder at Gwen. Then the music changed and the Bunheads sprang forward to begin the maypole dance.

"So long, suckers!" Rocky shouted.

The maypole was set center stage and each villager grabbed one of the colored ribbons. Then they formed a wide circle and began to weave their ribbons around the pole.

"As soon as this dance is over, our lives are finished," Mary Bubnik moaned.

"I can't believe I'm spending my last few minutes of freedom hiding behind a Styrofoam rock," Gwen grumbled. "I should have been at Hi Lo's, eating my last dinner of ice cream, candy, and cake."

"That's not dinner," Rocky commented. "That's dessert."

"It's *my* last meal," Gwen shot back. "And I can eat what I want."

"Would you two quit arguing?" Zan whispered. "I'm trying to think."

"Don't hurt yourself," Gwen muttered.

"Think of what?" McGee asked.

"A way out of this mess."

"What way?" Gwen looked off into the wings. "Every way out of here leads right into a policeman's arms. Unless we decided to run out through the audience, which would be really embarrassing."

Zan shook her head. "I'm trying to think of a way to prove that Thaddeus Taylor is our Monster."

"How?" Rocky asked. "That guy is long gone. And the only proof we had were a couple of spots of glow paint on his shoes, and a little of Miss Delacorte's birdseed in his left cuff."

McGee was lying with her chin resting on the floor, listening glumly to her friends talk. Things looked hopeless. She turned her head toward the base of the fountain with a sigh.

Something rustled in the wall close by her head. McGee held her breath and stared intently at the fake stones lining the fountain.

Two eyes peered back at her through the crack in front of her face. They blinked and McGee nearly fainted. She tried to move her lips to speak, but only a tiny rasp came out.

"He's . . . not . . . gone," McGee croaked.

"Who?" Rocky asked.

"Thad!" McGee finally found her voice. "He's right here. *In* the fountain!"

"The fountain?" Gwen stood straight up and this time she didn't care who saw her. The only thing separating her from the Monster of Mulberry Avenue was a plywood wall covered in Styrofoam rocks, and she wasn't about to stick around. Unfortunately, her bat cape snagged on the rocks and she couldn't budge an inch. "Heeeeeeeeeelp!"

Her cry startled everyone — the villagers in the maypole dance, the rest of the gang — but most of all, it scared Thaddeus Taylor, who leaped up out of the fountain as if he'd been stung by a bee.

Rocky shouted, "Grab him!"

Thaddeus tried to leap over the wall, but his foot tripped over one of the fake bushes and he fell right beside Gwen, who sat down heavily on his chest with a loud "Ooomph!"

Excited murmurs came from the audience. Everyone was wondering if all this action was actually part of the ballet. The orchestra members hesitated, unsure of what to do, and the conductor motioned for them to keep on playing.

"Hurry, do your bat movements," Zan whispered out of the corner of her mouth. "We have to get that maypole!"

McGee and Rocky caught on to Zan's plan immediately and, waving their arms up and down, swooped over to the village dancers, who had stopped dancing completely.

Rocky grabbed hold of the brightly decorated pole and barked, "Give me that."

The boy holding up the pole was so confused by what was happening that he handed it over without question.

"Don't," Courtney protested. "She's just trying to ruin our dance."

Rocky rolled her eyes and murmured, "Get real." McGee, Zan, and Mary Bubnik scooped up the dangling ribbons while Rocky carried the pole over toward the fountain, where Thad was struggling to shove Gwen off his chest. With a mighty heave he pushed her aside and leaped to his feet, only to find a swarm of dancing bats around him.

"The police are here," Zan hissed. She repeated some lines from a Tiffany Truenote novel to convince him. "They know all about you. I suggest you cooperate and maybe they'll give you time off for good behavior."

"What?" Thad squinted off into the wings to see if what she had said was true. Rocky rushed in and, kneeling down low, held the pole close to the guard as the other three raced in a circle around him, wrapping the ribbons around his body. Before the guard knew what had happened, they had pinned his arms down to his sides. Rocky stepped back out of the way and cried, "Gotcha!"

The music cue sounded for Dracula's triumphal entrance and Armand Van Valkenberg came onto the stage from the wings. The boys from St. Luke's in their bat costumes fluttered around him like an aerial escort.

Tyson and Joel did their bat moves over to the girls and whispered, "Way to go!"

"What are you guys doing?" McGee demanded. "You're not in this dance."

"We are now," Joel replied.

"Armand told us to get Thad off the stage, any way we can," Tyson explained. "And that's exactly what we're going to do."

With a grin, Tyson gave the bewildered guard a strong push. Since he was tied to the pole, he couldn't keep his balance and he fell over backwards. Joel and Clint caught one end of the pole before Thaddeus hit the ground. Then Tyson, with

Rocky's help, bent down and picked up the other end. They lifted the pole onto their shoulders and the guard looked like a side of beef ready to be barbecued on a spit.

Then Armand made it all look like part of the ballet. With a grand gesture, he pointed toward the wings and cried, "Take him away! He will be burned at the stake at midnight."

Rocky nodded and whispered, "Okay, bats, let's dance this joker off the stage."

As the boys from St. Luke's and Rocky carried the pole toward the wings, Gwen, Mary Bubnik, Zan, and McGee raised their arms and performed their best bat dance ever. It would have been quite frightening, had they not been grinning from ear to ear.

Detective Pinskey was waiting backstage with his men. Zan quickly plucked the Polaroid picture out of Thad's pocket and then motioned for Rocky and the boys to set their captive down in front of the amazed policemen.

"Here you go, Sergeant," Zan said proudly. "Here's your Monster of Mulberry Avenue. We have evidence to prove it."

"So do we," the detective said, gesturing for the two officers to handcuff Thaddeus and take him away. Then Detective Pinskey turned to Zan and said the words she had been waiting her whole life to hear.

"Thank you, young lady," he said, bowing slightly. "You've just saved the city of Deerfield a lot of trouble."

He didn't *exactly* say that she had saved an entire town, but it was close enough. Zan wrapped her arms around her friends and whispered, "This is the happiest day of my life."

Chapter Fourteen

That Sunday, forty costumed guests converged on the McGee farmhouse outside Deerfield for the big Halloween party. Rocky, Gwen, and Mary Bubnik were hanging out by the snack table in the kitchen while McGee waited for Zan, who was late.

"This party is a megahit!" Rocky shouted over the music blaring from the sound system in the living room. She was dressed as a Ninja, with black karate clothes and a face mask; a red scarf was tied around her forehead.

"No kidding," Gwen agreed, scooping up a large blob of onion dip with a potato chip. "The food's excellent."

"Boy, this is really uncomfortable," Mary Bubnik muttered. She was trying to find a way to sit down in her pink bunny rabbit costume. The tail, a huge, white pom-pom, made a big lump beneath her rear no matter which way she positioned herself on the chair.

"If it's so uncomfortable, how come you decided to wear it?" Gwen remarked, stuffing another chip in her mouth.

"My mom made this for me three years ago, and she insists I wear it. It's the only thing she ever sewed," Mary Bubnik replied. "Besides, I won first prize for it in the Kiwanis Halloween contest two years running."

Rocky squinted at Gwen's costume and asked, "Now tell me once again, what are you?"

Gwen bit loudly into her chip. "I'm a farmer." Gwen was wearing a pair of denim overalls, a red plaid flannel shirt, an old straw hat, and her brother Jay's heavy work boots.

"Why'd you choose something so . . . so regular?" Mary asked.

"Because I found the perfect trick-or-treat bag to go with it," Gwen explained. She went through the kitchen door onto the back porch and rolled in a rusty old wheelbarrow. "See? It can hold a lot of candy but, because it's part of my costume, no one will think I'm greedy. Plus, I don't have to wear out my arm lugging a heavy bag all over town."

Suddenly, the swinging door from the dining room opened and McGee stuck her head inside. She'd come as an astronaut and was wearing a jumpsuit, with matching sneakers, and mittens. Her dad had sprayed the entire outfit with silver paint the night before. The helmet she wore had a glass bubble face mask with NASA written on the sides; there was matching lettering on the back of her jumpsuit.

"Are you guys ready for this?" McGee said, flipping up her face mask. "Courtney is about to make her announcement."

"She is?" Rocky exclaimed, as the girls leaped to their feet.

"Have the boys from St. Luke's arrived?" Mary Bubnik asked.

"They just walked in the door," Zan said, coming into the room behind McGee. She looked just like a gypsy fortune-teller in her swirling peasant skirt and puffy-sleeved blouse with a colorful scarf tied around her head. Long, gold loops dangled from her earlobes, and her forearms jangled with bracelets. Zan smiled mysteriously and said, "And you'll never believe who's with them."

"Who?" Gwen asked.

"Armand Van Valkenberg!"

"Dracula?" Mary Bubnik gasped. "I thought he'd never speak to us again after what happened during the ballet."

"Armand told me that he's had to perform this role so many times, it was nice to have a little change in it," Zan said.

"He said it put some real excitement into his life," McGee added.

"That's putting it mildly," Rocky cracked.

"Even Mr. Anton isn't too mad," McGee went on. "The ballet got lots of publicity from all of this. Besides, he's just glad that Elmer Tillotson was captured."

"Elmer Tillotson?" Gwen arched a skeptical eyebrow. "Who is that?"

"Thaddeus Taylor," Zan replied. "Alias Proctor Phelps, alias Simon Stubbs, alias Bert Bellows. The police say he's responsible for a list of crimes as long as his arm. I'd say he'll be behind bars for quite a long time."

"They figured all that out in one day?" Mary Bubnik asked.

Zan shook her head. "Detective Pinskey had been watching our theatre for a long time. He had everyone checked out on Thursday and found out all that information about Thad. That's why he showed up at the theatre."

"But there's one thing I never did figure out," Mary Bubnik remarked. "How did Thad, uh, Elmer, make himself look so tall?"

"The same way we did," Zan said with a grin. "It turns out that he actually *does* have a wife, and she was the one who would sit on his shoulders. Then, after booing their victims, they'd split apart and walk down the street like any normal couple, with his wife wearing the stolen purse on her arm."

"Wow!" Rocky exclaimed. "That's amazing."

"I believe we can truly say that the case is finally closed," Zan declared.

"Not quite," McGee said, with a mischievous gleam in her eyes. "Aren't we forgetting something?"

"What?" Mary Bubnik asked.

"The bet!" Gwen shouted. "And Courtney's announcement!"

"Come on, you guys," Rocky said, rubbing her hands together. "I want to be real close so I can see her face when she tells everyone that we're the best dancers in our class."

Gwen took a last bite of dip and said thoughtfully, "You know, I never dreamed that revenge would feel so great."

Still laughing, they trooped out into the crowded living room. Courtney was standing silently in the corner, not talking to anyone. She still had her coat on. Page and Alice looked equally miserable.

"May I have your attention, everyone?" McGee said, clapping her hands together. Once the hubbub had died down, she declared, "Courtney Clay has an important announcement she'd like to make."

The room of costumed people clutching cups of punch and slices of pizza turned to stare at Courtney, who was blushing to the roots of her hair. She cleared her throat awkwardly. "Um, Katie McGee and I had a little bet, you see, and well, uh . . ."

Courtney glanced over at the boys from St. Luke's, who had been playing the Nintendo game on the television, but now were watching her curiously.

"She won. And I'd just like to say . . ." Courtney took a deep breath that seemed to start at the end of her toes and work its way up her entire body. But before she could say another word, McGee stepped forward and put her hand on Courtney's arm.

"That's okay, Courtney," McGee whispered. "You don't have to say it."

Courtney exhaled sharply and stared at McGee in confusion. "Then why did you . . . ?"

"I just wanted to see if you would." McGee turned back to the party and announced, "Courtney just wanted to tell you that we'll all be gathering in the old barn across the street to form teams to go on a super-duper haunted treasure hunt!"

A cheer went up from the kids and they raced for

the front door, leaving a bewildered Courtney standing in the middle of the room. After a second, Page and Alice joined their friend and the Bunheads hurried after the rest of the crowd.

"What came over you?" Rocky demanded, marching up to McGee. "Why didn't you let her say it?"

"Because — " McGee quickly checked to make sure that everyone else had left her living room. Then she lowered her voice and whispered, "Because if Courtney Clay announced that we are the best dancers at the Academy, what do you think people would do?"

Gwen shoved her glasses up on her nose. "They'd laugh."

"Exactly." McGee crossed her arms across her chest. "Nobody would believe her, and we would all look ridiculous."

Mary Bubnik giggled happily. "Instead, the boys from St. Luke's came to *our* party."

"Courtney admitted total defeat," Gwen said with a grin.

"*And* — !"

Rocky held up the front page of the *Deerfield Times*. There was a picture of all of them standing beside Detective Pinskey, who was shaking Zan's hand.

"The whole town thinks Zan is the best detective in the world!" Rocky crowed, patting Zan on the back.

The five friends beamed at each other. Outside they could hear cries of delight as the party guests received their maps for the treasure hunt. For a whole minute, none of them spoke. They just held hands while little tears of joy appeared at the corners of their eyes.

"What's everybody getting so mushy for?" Rocky finally blurted out. "Come on. We've got a treasure hunt to win!"

Bad News Ballet

Coming soon:
#10 A Dog Named Toe Shoe

The animal-control officer pulled out an official-looking pad. "According to a Mrs. Clay, this dog bit her daughter less than an hour ago."

"O'Rourke didn't bite Courtney!" Gwen shouted.

"O'Rourke?" the other officer repeated. "You said this dog's name is Oscar Einstein."

"Well, his full name is T-Bone Oscar Eddie Slick Hoover O'Rourke Einstein," Mary said, "um, but we all call him . . ."

Zan suddenly blurted out, "Toe Shoe."

"Well," the red-faced dog catcher said, "we have to get this mutt out of here."

Toe Shoe let out a sharp yelp as they dragged him over the threshold into the corridor.

"Poor doggie," Mary Bubnik's eyes welled up with tears. "They're taking Toe Shoe to jail, and he may never get out."

"We'll get him out." Rocky slammed her fist into her palm. "I don't care if we have to drag Courtney to the pound and put her there in his place — he's getting out."

America's Favorite Series

THE BABY-SITTERS CLUB

by Ann M. Martin

Collect Them All!

The seven girls at Stoneybrook Middle School get into all kinds of adventures...with school, boys, and, of course, baby-sitting!

☐ MG41588-3	Baby-sitters on Board! Super Special #1	$2.95
☐ MG41583-2	#19 Claudia and the Bad Joke	$2.75
☐ MG42004-6	#20 Kristy and the Walking Disaster	$2.75
☐ MG42005-4	#21 Mallory and the Trouble with Twins	$2.75
☐ MG42006-2	#22 Jessi Ramsey, Pet-sitter	$2.75
☐ MG42007-0	#23 Dawn on the Coast	$2.75
☐ MG42002-X	#24 Kristy and the Mother's Day Surprise	$2.75
☐ MG42003-8	#25 Mary Anne and the Search for Tigger	$2.75
☐ MG42419-X	Baby-sitters' Summer Vacation Super Special #2	$2.95
☐ MG42503-X	#26 Claudia and the Sad Good-bye	$2.95
☐ MG42502-1	#27 Jessi and the Superbrat	$2.95
☐ MG42501-3	#28 Welcome Back, Stacey!	$2.95
☐ MG42500-5	#29 Mallory and the Mystery Diary	$2.95
☐ MG42499-8	Baby-sitters' Winter Vacation Super Special #3	$2.95
☐ MG42498-X	#30 Mary Anne and the Great Romance	$2.95
☐ MG42497-1	#31 Dawn's Wicked Stepsister	$2.95
☐ MG42496-3	#32 Kristy and the Secret of Susan	$2.95
☐ MG42495-5	#33 Claudia and the Mystery of Stoneybrook	$2.95
☐ MG42494-7	#34 Mary Anne and Too Many Boys	$2.95
☐ MG42508-0	#35 Stacey and the New Kids on the Block	$2.95

For a complete listing of all the Baby-sitter Club titles write to :
Customer Service at the address below.

Available wherever you buy books...or use the coupon below.

Scholastic Inc. P.O. Box 7502, 2932 E. McCarty Street, Jefferson City, MO 65102

Please send me the books I have checked above. I am enclosing $_____

(please add $2.00 to cover shipping and handling). Send check or money order–no cash or C.O.D.'s please

Name_____

Address_____

City_____ State/Zip_____

Please allow four to six weeks for delivery. Offer good in U.S.A. only. Sorry, mail order not available to residents of Canada. Prices subject to change.   BSC 789